PRAISE FOR

A must read for lovers of Samurai adventures.

— *Hon Baka*

Spot on and real.

— *Stella Myers*

I highly recommend Cold Blood and I for one am eagerly awaiting the next book.

— *Carlyle Clark, Heroines of Fantasy*

Lawrence's descriptive skills struck me especially. . . . Yamabuki is a wonderful character, and she is coming of age just before a ruinous war in Japan.

— *Anne Vonhof*

I was torn between wanting to race through the story to find out what happened next and wanting to linger over the tale, savoring the exotic and the unusual.

— *C.R.*

Cold Rain

BOOKS BY
KATHERINE M. LAWRENCE

COLD SAKÉ

SWORD OF THE TAKA SAMURAI series
COLD BLOOD
COLD RAIN
*COLD HEART**
*COLD TRAIL**
*COLD FIRE**
*COLD STEEL**
*COLD FATE**

*THE BROKEN LAND**

* Coming Soon

冷雨

REIU

Cold Rain

Yamabuki and the Warlord Prince

Sword of the Taka Samurai
Book Two

Katherine M. Lawrence

Toot Sweet Ink

tootsweet.ink

Boulder

A Toot Sweet Ink Book
Published by Toot Sweet Inc.
6525 Gunpark Drive Suite 370
Boulder, CO 80301

Visit us at tootsweet.ink

Toot Sweet Ink is a trademark of Toot Sweet Inc.

Library of Congress Control Number: 2015957685
First Edition

ISBN: 978-1-943194-04-9 (hardback)
ISBN: 978-1-943194-03-2 (trade paper)
ISBN: 978-1-943194-05-6 (ePub)

To LS

ACKNOWLEDGMENTS

I want to thank all those who helped bring this novel to life. Gratitude goes to Tonia Hurst and Anne Vonhof for their insights on early drafts. I also would like to thank Jane Campbell of the Bonsai Crit Group, Rocky Mountain Fiction Writers Crit Group leader Lesley Smith, and members Paige Danes and Jane Bigelow for their excellent feedback and comments.

As always, I want to thank my indefatigable editor and publisher extraordinaire, Laura Scott, for her editing, art direction, and abilities as a layout maven, and whose Zen-like understanding of the *Chicago Manual of Style*, 16th edition, pulled all my scribblings together into a unified whole.

For any errors, omissions, or problems with the text, I take all responsibility for such shortcomings.

CONTENTS

Long before it was called Japan,
the island empire was known
to the world as Akitsushima,
the Autumn Creek Land,
and among its samurai,
one of its mightiest warriors was
a woman named Yamabuki.

Cold Rain

Spring 1172:
Known as Year of the Metal Rabbit,
Second Year of Shōan,
eight years prior to the Genpei War
and the ensuing struggle
for the mastery of Japan
that tore the realm apart
and ushered in the era of the warlords.

ONE

FEMALE WARRIORS WERE ORDERED TO BEAUTIFY THEMSELVES

COLD RAIN WASHED runnels of blood past her feet. She had never been in an actual duel; never had anyone fallen before her sword. Three dead bodies lay in the road. Her palms still pulsed from the impact of steel against steel. The dying echoes of the assassins' screams lingered in her ears, mixing with the ever-increasing beat of the wind-driven rain. The skies turned black. Thunder rolled through the forest. The temperature dropped.

Even as icy showers drenched everything, she still felt flush. Rain soaked her hair. She mopped her brow. Cold entered her armor where her chest protector was torn. She touched her own breasts. The fencing master's blade had only split the corselet's outer layer. The imperial yellow under-silk remained intact. No blood. Not so much as a nick.

She wiped her cheek, fingering the single wound she received in the fray. It was viscid. Only when she touched it did it sting. Her naked fingertips extending from her sleeve-and-hand armor were now red. She let the *reiu* wash away the blood.

She had to get Mochizuki out of the ice storm. She took the

colt's bridle, leading him to a sheltered place under the trees. His hot breath steamed. She looked into his dark-brown, moonlike eyes. "You never doubted I'd survive, did you?" Impassively the colt looked back at her.

Her breathing had almost returned to normal.

The rain and hail increased, drenching the dead, pelting them with pearl-white ice pebbles. The cloudburst grew so thick it became a fog. But like any fury, it abated. The rains began to die away. The grayness lifted. High clouds broke. The bright skies of noon shined through.

A piercing screech rose from the nearby Shintō shrine. A black kite perched on one of the crossbeams of the red *torii* entrance gate.

"A *tonbi*. Has he been watching us?"

Though usually not superstitious, she took comfort in the bird. A good omen. Kites were kin to *taka*. Taka: "hawk," her clan name.

The bird's gold-speckled eyes peered first at her, and then at the dead. As if agitated, it swiveled its head from side to side. Now left, then right, not able to make up its mind. It straightened itself. Shrieked. Then, beating its wings six or seven times, it flew up over the forest and soared into the blueness of the clearing sky. Giving forth a final prolonged and chilling cry, the tonbi disappeared.

"You know, Mochizuki, it's said kites carry fallen warriors' spirits into the next world." It was an ancient Taka clan belief—older than Shintō, going back to an age when spiritual matters were the province of female shamans. "The tonbi flew west," she said. "The Red Land lies beyond the setting sun."

The kite might possibly have flown off to the Western Paradise with the essences of the dead, but the bodies still lay where they fell. Though she had seen bodies before, until today she had never seen one decapitated.

Her father's retainers sometimes argued with an almost ghoulish relish, trying to sound jaundiced, about the fine points of "taking the head." A head was proof that a warlord's foe was truly dead. An entire warrior lore had grown up around the "proper" way to cut off the head of a foe. It was an art. A head could not be allowed to putrefy. A bad smell was a breach of good manners. There were heated debates whether to use salt or saké as a preservative; salt dried out the face, but saké bloated the features.

The gruesome punctilios were sedulously followed by the Taka, not only in anticipation of victory but also in the case of their own deaths. Before a major battle, samurai were admonished to wash, oil, comb, and perfume their hair so that the smell of rotted flesh would not offend should their severed heads happen to be presented to their enemies. So that no one would suffer the humiliation of being taken for a girl, those whose facial hair was a fine fuzz were told to stain their beards and moustaches with darkening cream.

As for female warriors, they were ordered to beautify themselves.

Yamabuki imagined what might have happened had the assassins succeeded: Standing over her body, daggers drawn, they would be cutting her head away from her neck, ready to immerse it into some awful kill-box. She pictured her skull, dangling by its long black tresses, as the ninja lowered it into the liquid-filled canister. The saké, now tinged red by her blood, would slowly rise up under her chin, coming up to her gaping mouth and lips. As they lowered the head further, the liquid would move over her cheeks and cover her vacant eyes . . . until it closed around her forehead and her scalp as the last of her finally disappeared beneath the fluid. Only her hair would be left floating on the surface. And then the lid would be closed, sealing her in darkness.

She shuddered and then scoffed at herself for her overly vivid imaginings. The ninja had no kill-box with them. It had been an ambush, not a battle. And it wasn't her head that they were after, it was the dispatches she carried.

She put her mailed hand into her sleeve. Her bare fingers found the three scrolls, each wound about a jade spool, and, in turn, each sheathed inside a thick silk wrapping—a protective and decorative husk. Untouched.

Not so her blade, whose edge was now pitted by nicks and scuffs and smeared with blood. Gone was the luster that swordsmith Yukiyasu had polished into it.

She raised Tiger Claw and found her eyes in the reflection of the blade. Had her eyes changed? She never could have imagined any of this when she was summoned to Lady Taka's chamber just fourteen days before.

Two
FUJIWARA, THE MOST
ROYAL OF BLOOD

A HARD COLD RAIN FELL. The brazier was dead. The room, totally dark. Chilly.

"Mother wants to see me?" Yamabuki mumbled, still half-wrapped in the bedding.

"*Hai*," Tomoko answered through the closed panel door. "Rei's standing right here . . . to accompany you."

A crack in the door let in a sliver of flickering light. Tomoko must have brought a soya-oil lamp with her. Its distinctive odor insinuated itself throughout the room.

"What time is it?"

"First Watch. Hour of the Dog," Hanaye answered.

Both of my handmaids? And Rei here to escort me? This must be important.

"Isn't this late for an audience?" Yamabuki complained, knowing that there was nothing to do about it but to get ready. "Where does she wish to see me?"

"Her audience chamber." Tomoko paused, then asked, "May we enter?"

"Hai!" Yamabuki's tone was more filled with resignation than invitation.

Tomoko slid the door aside but the two handmaids remained standing at the threshold. Tomoko raised the lamp in one hand and peered in. Hanaye stood right behind her.

"Maybe you were having *good* dreams?" Tomoko giggled. "Sorry if I interrupted them."

"I don't think I was dreaming," Yamabuki muttered, still too sleepy to appreciate the sly humor. She swept her arm, indicating that the handmaids were to enter.

Tomoko and Hanaye slipped into the room. The lamplight lit up the chamber, throwing shadows into the corners.

Yamabuki, still in her bed, asked, "Did Rei say why my mother needs to see me?"

Tomoko shook her head. "Rei didn't seem very worried if that's what you mean. The compound's completely quiet. But you know your mother—she doesn't sleep when she has something on her mind."

"How cold is it?" Yamabuki kicked the quilts aside and slowly stood up.

"Rainy spring night. Three kimono, no more."

"Please help me," Yamabuki said.

Hanaye already carried three formal kimono layers for the occasion. She and Tomoko immediately helped Yamabuki out of her bedclothes and into the garments.

"Full make-up?" Yamabuki asked, already knowing the answer.

"Yes," Tomoko answered. "So I am told."

Yamabuki exhaled.

Within a quarter hour, Yamabuki followed Rei, who walked

with a raised soya-oil lamp down the long mizmaze hallways that led to the easternmost estate house.

Yamabuki knew this route well. It took her from her westernmost estate house, through a few interior hallways, but mostly outside along covered wooden walkways open to the air. She passed ten other large houses before reaching the largest estate house, where her parents lived.

The spring rains drummed on the roofs. Water gurgled as it entered the garden pools. A fog heavy with the scent of the sea wandered across the grounds of the compound. The night air invigorated and brought her fully awake.

When she arrived at her mother's audience chamber, Rei slid the panels apart. Inside, under the light of at least ten braziers, Yamabuki's mother, wearing formal but festive spring robes, sat on a small dais.

Yamabuki stepped through the doorway and kowtowed. "*Denka*," she said—*Your majesty*—her forehead touching the floor planks. Rei, just outside the doors, pulled the panels closed with a clunk. Mother and daughter were alone.

Though she came before her mother, who was still young, the orange flickering fires made her look like a Buddha.

"Get up," her mother said with a small wave of the hand. "We can dispense with formalities now that it's just us."

Yamabuki slid into a sitting posture.

Without any of the usual pleasantries, her mother began, "Your father tells me that you are to embark on a period of *musha shugyō*."

Yamabuki's heart leapt. "I was not aware of this."

"Yes," her mother continued, "and he is also aware that I might not be *too* happy about the idea of exposing you to the dangers of traveling by yourself for a year, maybe even two. You have hardly seen sixteen springs."

"It will be seventeen years by Sōkō," Yamabuki said with contained excitement.

"The time of the Descent of Frost?" Her mother took in a deep breath and shook her head. "That is seven months from now!" She hardly hid her exasperation. "Right now it's barely the time of the Grain Rain. The crops are not even in the ground and you are speaking as if the coming winter was almost upon us."

Her mother held her mouth tight and was talking fast, all at the same time. Yamabuki knew to tread lightly.

"I must say I am surprised . . . and not surprised," Lady Taka continued, absentmindedly drumming her fingers against the floor. "I knew that if you persisted in these"—she paused, almost faltering—"*martial* studies that it would come to this though I didn't expect it *this* soon. Not for another two years. Foolish me. Foolish me to think that maybe by now you'd have the wisdom to find a husband and settle down and have some children like the daughter of a *daimyō* that you are."

"But mother," said Yamabuki, trying not to sound plaintive, "you were a whole year *younger* than I am now when you rode out on *your* musha shugyō."

Lady Taka's eyes flashed and not in a good way. "Those were different times, and even then, it changed me . . . and not necessarily for the better."

"I shall return alive. I'm well trained. I shall come back *alive*."

"Ha!" Lady Taka let out a deep sigh. "That you will return *alive* I have little doubt, nor does your father, or he would not be sending you on this journey. But you do not understand what musha shugyō means. Those two years, it's what they take *away* from you. It's *meant* to change you and it changes you in ways that you cannot know nor can it be undone. It's only afterward—" She broke off, shaking her head, her mouth closed tight.

Yamabuki, still sitting, bowed and nodded.

Her mother continued, "You are now truly of marriageable age. Most men of standing do not want to marry warriors, even female ones."

"Father married you."

"I said *most* men, and besides, it was an arranged marriage that would seal a peace between our clans—a seal of common blood. *You.*" Though she did not point, she might as well have. "There's as much Itō blood—four hundred years of a noble lineage that flows from the Fujiwara, the most *royal* of blood, my blood—that's in your veins. As much Itō blood as Taka blood." Lady Taka pointed to the two distinct roundel *mon* that graced her own kimono. "The crossed twin-arrow feathers and the sign of the crescent moon are your heritage. You represent the union of two houses." She raised her arm with a sweep. The kimono fluttered. The roundels almost trembled.

"But there are others who can be married off," Yamabuki answered softly.

"Married off, is it?" She stared straight at her daughter.

Yamabuki shifted uneasily at her mother's displeasure.

Her mother said, "Indeed, and of all the children, including the boys, you are the *only* one who has taken it into her head to follow this path. Prince Tachibana is always pushing Atsumichi forward, trying to get his son a good marital match—a politically astute one."

Yamabuki smirked. "Tongue boy."

"Don't laugh. This is serious."

"I know, mother," Yamabuki said with contrition.

"I should hope you do."

"If I marry, I can never do as I please. If I have babies, then I'll have to stay here to supervise their care. I shall never make my journey to Kara, or visit the lands of the Sòng Dynasty."

"Travel across the Leeward Sea! Are these the kinds of insanities that Nakagawa is putting into your head?"

"No! It's my idea and one which I shall fulfill," Yamabuki insisted, unable to keep from raising her nose.

Lady Taka looked heavenward, then back at Yamabuki. "We need someone to produce an heir and not some willful wanderer who thinks nothing of her obligations."

Yamabuki bowed, her forehead briefly touching the planking.

"I can see I made a mistake to let you grow up so free."

"*Gomen nasai.*" Yamabuki bowed yet again.

"No. No. You should not be sorry. It is *I* who should be sorry. Your father always gets his way." She paused as she brought up a calm from deep within herself and sighed. "A daimyō always gets his way, even if he is also a husband," she whispered to herself.

"Gomen nasai," Yamabuki said crisply so there could be no mistake about her sincerity, deeply apologizing, her face against the floor.

"Sit up," her mother commanded. "Tell me why you are so set against marriage. You're a woman. You *do* like men . . . or is it, with all your warrior inclinations, that you happen to like . . ." She bit her lip, leaving the rest unsaid.

"No. No. I do. I like men. I like them well enough."

"Well, it would not matter if you didn't. It is always better when you love the man, but even if you did not, there is more to think about than yourself. All the rest of that can come after." She sighed again, visibly trying to contain her exasperation.

"I'm afraid of what is to become of me if I stay here," Yamabuki said softly.

"It's not a bad life."

"I know. Nakagawa once said that, and when he did, I knew he was repeating what you think." Yamabuki continued, "But life here makes me no more than a bird in a cage."

"You consider *me* a caged bird, daughter?"

Yamabuki looked down. "No, mother," she whispered very softly.

Lady Taka shook her head and again drummed the floor with her fingers. "You know: I hear myself in you. I said the very same things to my mother . . . and my father."

"Then you know that I am right."

"No. I know that you are *young*. You do not know where you are right and where you are wrong. Alas, you cannot understand where you are wrong until after it is too late. After it is finished. Such is the nature of life."

"But in the end the Itō clan let you go on musha shugyō, did they not?"

Lady Taka nodded without a word. Then, her voice soft, she said, "I don't have to remind *you* for what a warrior trains, do I?"

Yamabuki shook her head in agreement. "I understand very well."

"Once again, you do and you don't. It is to fight. And fighting in the world is as real as real can be. You say you will return from your journey alive, so chances are that someone else will not, and they will pay the price of blood."

Yamabuki nodded. "Nakagawa and I have talked of this."

"Yes, but *you and I* have *not*." Lady Taka continued softly. "Everyone is different. Men and women are different."

Yamabuki nodded.

"In matters of the heart, a man is different from a woman, no?" Yamabuki slowly nodded. *What is she saying?*

"The body has only one heart. Love springs from the same heart as does fighting spirit. And men, for the most part, take matters of the heart less seriously. For them, it's all dyed in glory. They brag. This goes for matters of love as much as matters of battle. All for show.

"A woman, on the other hand, may experience matters of the heart—the passion of love or the heat of a fight—quite differently than most men. If it comes to combat on the road, I say that you must do your best. You *must* prevail. That is the *only* allowable outcome. And once you have fought, you will find yourself alone. Neither your father, Nakagawa, nor I, nor anyone who you can truly trust will be there to offer you solace. Afterward, it is something you will bear alone."

"I understand."

"Actually you do not, but there is no way around it. For all your training and for all you have been taught, you have also been sheltered. All girls are sheltered, even tough ones." Her mother smiled wistfully and sadly, all at the same time. "No Taka boy would dare start in with you. They *know* who you are."

"I can handle them." Yamabuki's eyes flashed.

"Indeed you can and could. And you know them. All of you grew up together, even though most were not of your station. Out on the road, a stranger comes along: A beggar might turn out to be a master of weapons. A samurai may whimper like a coward if you stand up to him. A pretty woman might put a dagger in your back when you look the other way. You needn't be unduly frightened, but you should not let your woman's heart always see the best in others.

"You know that I have tried to carry seven babies into this world."

Seven?

"You were the third and the only one who lived past four springs. You had two older brothers, you know." She paused. "The others? I think there were two girls and a boy and one so soon it could not be determined. And you, the third child to whom I gave birth, have grown up tall and strong and quite bright for your age." She gave her daughter a small smile. "Everyone said that since you were a girl you would not amount to much. Imagine, telling a mother that!" She laughed softly. "You do know the karmic burden I have carried and now that karma has been passed to you."

Yamabuki looked at her mother, questioningly.

"Meaning," she continued, "if you do not have a brother, then *you* must be the one to bear a male heir to carry on the Taka-Itō lineage. But by going through musha shugyō, you are putting not only yourself at risk but staking the destiny of the Taka, and tangling all of it in your quest."

Yamabuki started to protest, wanting to say that all would be well, but her mother would not let her interrupt. "No. No. I do not need to hear from you. You need to hear from *me*. For all my protestations, I am resigned, for I have sat in the same sort of place as where you now sit. I too heard my mother's words float to my ears but not touch them."

Lady Taka took a deep breath. "You will leave four days from now. That should give you enough time to prepare."

Yamabuki was taken aback, trying not to show any hesitation that might be interpreted as reluctance and, therefore, a reason to abandon the plans altogether. "I will be ready," she said with confidence.

"I am told you will be asked to carry a dispatch from your father to the Taka Palace in Heian-kyō. Now," she said, putting a hand into her sleeve, "I also have something I want you to take with you." She produced something the size of a dagger that was wrapped in rough silk that was the indigo color of the Taka clan. Quickly she splayed it open, taking off the silk in the way a mother might undo the clothing of her baby, revealing a scroll whose edge was sealed with dark-red wax bearing the Taka emblem.

Her mother lifted the rolled scroll as if it were an object of devotion. Its paper was wound tightly around a white jade spool. The scroll was husked by a magnificent stiff silk wrap of vivid colors—red, dark blue, but mostly golden yellow.

She exhaled. "This is to be delivered to my brother at the Itō Palace."

Yamabuki, still sitting before the dais, leaned forward, bowing to acknowledge that she understood the gravity of the undertaking.

"If you cannot deliver it, burn it."

THREE

CAN YOU KEEP A SECRET?

YAMABUKI EMERGED INTO the darkness outside her mother's chamber. Only a few lights illuminated the long hall: some candles in a cluster and two soya-oil lamps. Another light suddenly appeared. It started to move. Not sure who or what approached her, she paused.

"Rei?" Rei was nowhere to be found.

The light continued in her direction.

"Yamabuki?" It was Tomoko. "Is everything good?"

Yamabuki laughed softly, then gushed, "Beyond good!"

"I came to light your way back."

Yamabuki almost skipped. "Can you keep a secret?"

"Hai," Tomoko whispered.

Of course, she could. She always had. Yamabuki felt foolish for even asking. Quickly she went on, wanting nothing more than to share her glee. "I am going to go through musha shugyō."

"Musha shugyō?" Even by candlelight, she saw Tomoko's eyes grow wide. "That's *wonderful*," Tomoko stammered, then fell silent. A moment later, with a cheerful smile she asked, "When are you leaving?"

"Four days."

Yamabuki thought she heard Tomoko's voice quavering in response, "So soon?" Tomoko paused and then continued quickly, "I mean—I mean there's so much to be done. Just four days?"

Yamabuki cleared her throat. "Four days will be perfect. Tonight is probably my last time with the moon this month."

"Me too. You know we're the same on that," Tomoko said.

All royal houses have secrets and the Taka were no different. Secrets swelled and converged like streams coming down a mountain. Some followed their own course while most are fed by tributaries. That is how it was throughout the Empire. The loftier the personage, the more sources of rumor.

Rumors repeated in Ō-Utsumi came in all hues and stripes. Most of the gossip was ultimately harmless—idle and more or less innocuous. It consisted of reciting whose amorous eyes were on whom and what trysts were afoot. Romantic speculations.

A more serious form of gossip involved who was in favor in the Court and who was not. Whose advice was sought and whose was dismissed. Who was on the rise and who was in eclipse.

But there was also a more serious kind and this kind had to do with real power; the kind that people would kill for, and those secrets usually involve the warlord and those closest to him.

FOUR

RIVER OF FORTY THOUSAND SANDS

PLOTS CAN SPROUT SUDDENLY. Like all truly great opportunities, they come to life without warning. This one came two days earlier, when the Taka traitor's spies reported that Yamabuki was about to ride out, unaccompanied, heading for Heian-kyō, carrying two mysterious communiqués.

The traitor, who went by an alias, Yo-aki, which means "Strange Mystic," was one of the few who knew about the dispatches, but he did not know the specifics of the messages. In fact he had absolutely no idea of what they contained, and this bothered him greatly, for until that morning he had not been informed even of their existence. Had he fallen out of favor? The messages were in the form of sealed scrolls and they were handed directly from the mother and the father, respectively, to their daughter, and as far as Yo-aki could tell, from then on they were never out of Yamabuki's reach.

Yo-aki's master plan came to him in a flash. Not only would he get access to the scrolls by intercepting them, but he would also eliminate Yamabuki in a fell swoop. The scrolls were perhaps ultimately worthless. In any case, his curiosity would be satisfied. More important, Yamabuki would be eliminated.

Yo-aki never used intermediaries when he hired assassins. Mindful of the threat from counterspies, he met assassins personally, even though it exposed him to some danger. Ninja, not the most honorable people, might for various reasons make their own attempts on Yo-aki, but master swordsman that he was, he was likely better at killing than any of them were.

In fact, Yo-aki could have dispensed with assassins altogether and simply killed Yamabuki straightaway and practically at any time. He could have easily strangled her in her infancy, smothering her and then made it look like she had simply died in her sleep, just as her older brothers had. He was good at killing in a way that left no marks.

However, Yamabuki had never been the slightest threat to his plans, that is, until recently. Though it was clear that she had to die, she could not be allowed to fall under *anyone's* sword within the compound. Nothing that could in any way be linked back to him. She also could not even suddenly somehow fall sick, likely along with her food taster, and die unexpectedly of some mysterious ailment. That would not at all have suited Yo-aki's purposes. The deed had to be done by others and it had to happen far away from the Taka compound. Yamabuki, along with the scrolls, had to basically vanish and her body never found. Confusion as to her whereabouts, and swirling questions as to whether she was alive or dead, would suit Yo-aki's machinations.

And thus began Yo-aki's race by fast *kago* to the headwaters of the River of Forty Thousand Sands, to find a man known simply as Saburo, reputedly one of the most accomplished assassins in the Empire.

FIVE

THE MAN OF ICE

LOVE FADES. HATE ENDURES. That's what Saburo had come to believe. He had never killed anyone he loved, although he had killed some whom he hated. Mostly he killed those for whom he had no feelings whatever.

He sat before one hundred and sixty-seven funerary tablets inside the shrine he had erected in a private temple located within the grounds of his estate. The memorial tablets named all who fell before his sword, his knife, his arrow, his pike, his rope, or his bare hands. He was loath to resort to poisons or similar artifice. It was unmanly. His assassinations were based on attacking someone face-to-face. Poisons were more of a woman's fashion, all so the assassin didn't have to use her hands nor look into the eyes of her "object."

That was what Saburo had taken to calling his quarry: objects.

Though no doubt there were some women who enjoyed slaughter even more than many of their male counterparts did, rarely did they linger for the final throes. There were always some, however, who took particular relish in the performance of their acts. Some men and a few women of this singular profession were drawn to its practice for precisely this delight. However, Shima had been completely wrong in accusing Saburo of being one of those—someone who derives carnal excitement from killing. Saburo took no special relish in it. For him it was a matter of commerce and trade. It was simply what was. And it paid well.

People who came to his estate house brought money with them, willing to part with it for his discreet services. His patrons wanted the objects of their choosing dead, and their own identities kept secret.

Patrons. Saburo expected patronage and not an assassin's fee, though large sums of money were always passed to him at the beginning—"for expenses."

He made it a rule to never do any less than was required, but neither would he do any more. Killing was a business, so why take additional risk if there was no payment? And assassinating someone was always a risk in and of itself, for even a cornered rat will put up a fight, and you never knew which rat might have luck or chance on its side on the day it made its final stand.

There were times that Saburo became the target of others who wanted vengeance. That was why he slipped away once his assignment was completed—so that no one knew who had done the deed, something that also made him successful in his enterprise as well as favored by his patrons.

The handier and more efficient he proved himself, the more the rewards that flowed, so that over time Saburo lived as well as any Lord, but without the accompanying responsibilities. His estate befit royalty. Located just below the spring-fed headwaters of the River of Forty Thousand Sands, the site was carefully chosen, for here the river could be counted on to flow year round—even in the driest of summers, when many rivers turned into dirt, or in the coldest of winters when other rivers iced over. Part of the stream had been diverted to form a moat, part natural and part artificial, through a trench that bound ten large buildings. A high, thick stone wall ringed the grounds, hugging the moat of reeds and yellow rushes, where ducks and other aquatic fowl nested—natural guardians, for they were more reliable than dogs for making a disorderly commotion at the approach of strangers.

The trees that normally shaded lands as lavish as these were absent. All the approaches had long ago been logged off, leaving only open fields for the hundred or so paces from any direction.

Yet on the other side of the walls, all manner of trees thrived, drawing their moisture from the waters that ran beneath the property and the dark-brown soil that covered the grounds.

Saburo proved a complicated man with motives and behaviors that sometimes seemed at odds with an assassin's life. If he killed without feeling or remorse, why then did he pray for the souls of the dead—even for those whom he hated? Why build such an elaborate temple, with thick sliding double-panels made of hardwood, all to memorialize people he had killed?

When Saburo sealed himself inside the temple, his household staff knew he was not to be disturbed. There, Saburo sat in contemplation. Usually he chanted with his eyes completely closed, his head slightly bowed. The shrine, typical of most shrines in families possessing great wealth, was elegant in its simplicity—a set of riser-shelves, lacquered black, which held the arrayed funerary tablets, each tablet identical in size regardless of the deceased's rank or station. In death were all not equal? Each lozenge was about one hand high and each bore a name, though a wise assassin would not use an object's true name. Despite being a private shrine, if the authorities were somehow to get inside his bastion, the tablets would provide the intruders with a roster that connected Saburo to many cases of sudden or mysterious deaths or disappearances.

Thus the tablets were inscribed with death names, a Buddhist custom, which gave the departed a "precept" name. The names were conceived by Saburo without consulting a priest. Why get one involved? And, after all, Saburo had been a priest and he had never renounced his order. Thus, the afterlife names he chose were always appropriate.

The musty-sweet smoke of incense curled into the air and spread its aroma throughout the shrine. The scent was one from his days at the monastery. The perfumer who recreated it had said it was a reminder of the seasons, unified in a single expression: spring's plum blossoms, summer's lotus leaves, autumn's chrysanthemums, and winter's apricots. These four constituents, mixed with magnolia shavings to encourage steady burning, gave off the distinctive odor, bringing back with it memories, both painful and tender, of the monastery and its lessons.

The *tsurigane* resonated but a single time. Saburo sensed someone approaching. The floorboards creaked. A familiar step.

"Kiri?" Saburo called.

"Hai," answered a woman.

"Who summons me?" Saburo spoke without moving, the panel still shut.

"A stranger has come to the outer gates."

"Describe him," Saburo said without looking up.

"A lone samurai dressed in a simple cloak. He says he wants an audience."

Saburo opened his eyes. "Insignia?"

"None."

"Incognito, eh? If he needs it, clean him up. Then bring him to the audience room." The day had been warm and especially humid, unusually so for this time of year.

Saburo stood up, casting a long slow look across the *kami-dana*. About three-quarters of the tablet names were yet to be uttered. But they were all dead and the dead could wait. The living? They were another matter. Someone had come with a mission.

Saburo entered his private dressing chamber, where Kiri helped him don an outer robe of black silk. Though at first it seemed the robe bore no insignia or design, the perceptive eye could see the fine pinpoint stitching that revealed zodiac roundel designs. His robe black and his hair stark white created the contrast he sought—death itself moving in darkness. He put a black eye patch over his right eye to, among other things, give him an even more ominous look.

Before entering, Saburo looked into the audience chamber through an insubstantial void in the wall where he could appraise his guest, whom he guessed to be a man in his middle years. Saburo could tell his guest had gone to some trouble to dust-off this own garment, yet was not fully successful. It still carried the sheen of embedded grime. He had been on the road at least three days, probably more.

"Is he armed?" Saburo whispered to Kiri.

"A tachi and a personal sword," she whispered in reply. "He apologized for the dust. He said his kago was attacked by robbers and he walked the final leg of his trip."

Saburo inclined his ear, his signal that Kiri was to continue.

"There was a battle. Our guest survived. Everyone else fell."

"He get cut?"

"No, but his sword smells of blood."

"Who were his runners?"

"The Monkey Bunch," she whispered, almost a hiss. She raised her brow to say that this was something unusual.

"The Monkey Bunch? No one dares to takes them on. And then he survived and slayed the attackers powerful enough to do that? Unless he's a bluffer, he's most unusual."

Straightening himself, Saburo entered the audience chamber. The other man nodded slightly as though he were a daimyō acknowledging a vassal.

Saburo returned an equally vague bow.

Though the other man wore a cowl, Saburo could see his face more clearly. Skin smooth. Eyes dark. *A wolf, this one.*

"You've come to see me about something?" Saburo said softly, for it was up to those who sought Saburo's services to reveal themselves first.

The man pulled back his cowl, uncovering a dark, long mane of hair that gave him the look of a bear, a *kuma*. Certainly he was not as large as he seemed from his bearing, although he was by no means small.

Saburo's clients tended to be reticent about who they were, and there was something about this man that gave Saburo reason to believe details regarding his identity would not come easily. No matter. The only thing that had to be forthcoming was payment. For now, Saburo would simply call the stranger "Kuma."

"A courier is traveling up the North Road. She's headed for the capital and has two sealed scrolls."

Saburo listened.

"According to plan, she left two days ago taking the route through Chikuzen Prefecture. I have two ninja following her who will serve as informants and you can use them any way you want once you engage her."

Saburo continued listening.

"We want the scrolls with the seals intact."

"And the courier?"

"We want her dead."

"You said she has already left. From where?"

Kuma shifted imperceptibly. "Does it matter?"

"If I am to intercept her, it matters. She's coming through Chizuken, but what is her origin?"

The bear-man answered, "Far south."

"The clan?" he asked, even though he knew the answer. Better to keep Kuma talking.

Kuma cleared his throat. "Taka," he answered softly. "She's traveling as a samurai without badge of rank."

"Without badge of rank?"

Kuma nodded slowly.

"Her rank is not samurai?"

Kuma shook his head.

"A sham?" Kuma's expression showed he did not understand the point of the question, so Saburo prompted, "A handmaid? Someone untrained? A decoy?"

"She's trained."

"Trained how?"

"Trained in the *dojo*, but untested. Nothing outside the Taka compound," said Kuma.

Saburo's one good eye narrowed. "Trained *within* the compound?" he asked softly, his emphasis unmistakable.

Kuma nodded.

Saburo's one eye closed. *High rank.* The pieces were coming together—unspoken pieces that assassins never asked about, and which patrons never willingly revealed. "This woman? She is someone of status?" He was met by silence. "Of course she is. She's been trained in the compound."

Kuma nodded again.

"How old?

"Seventeen springs."

Saburo thought about all he'd heard and took a deep breath. He had decided: the one hundred and sixty-eighth object was about to be added to the tablets. From Ō-Utsumi, his object would have to cross at Kita. He had to leave this day by fast kago if he was going to kill her before she crossed the Barrier Strait and disappeared into the vastness of the Main Isle. "I will leave immediately."

Kuma nodded sharply. "No witnesses and no trace."

Six

PLUNGE A SHARP STEEL
PIKE INTO HER RIBS

S IX DAYS LATER, Saburo stood on Foot Trail above the cove at
the Barrier Strait. He had been waiting for Yamabuki since
first light. He had disguised himself with authentic crabber's at-
tire right down to the sandals from an actual crab fisher who was
delighted to part with the clothes off his back, along with a tightly woven wicker basket brimming with fresh-trapped crabs, for
thirty pieces of silver. All Saburo had to do was put on an old eye
patch that was made to look ragged and his disguise was complete—that and the black ink with which he dyed his hair.

Saburo situated himself halfway down the wooded bluff, lying
in wait with a steel pike. It was a lonely spot. Thus it was perfect.
It had a good vantage in both directions along the trail and also
had a clear view of the Strait and the cove far below.

The morning was warm and slightly hazy. The full-moon tide was
now rushing through the passage between the Isle of Unknown
Fires and Honshu.

Saburo placed the weapon just inside the crab basket, a place
where few would willingly thrust an exposed hand. When the

Taka girl walked by, all Saburo had to do was grab the pike, leap
at her, and plunge it into her ribs. Armor or not, the sharp-point-
ed steel would gore her. Because the pike would penetrate into
her lung cavity, it would almost instantly be fatal, for she would
be unable to breathe or make so much as a sound. He would tear
the *tantō* from out of his sleeve and slit her throat in one merciful
stroke, then quickly drag the body into the brush, leaving it for
the wild dogs.

At the moment, however, there was no one on the trail except
him. The morning remained unusually quiet, as if most everyone
had forgotten to wake up. Haul boats neither left nor arrived at
the cove. On most days by now, the shore would have been filled
with travelers at the foot of the bluffs. Today only the oystermen
with their buckets walked along the beaches.

The nearby town of Kita, too, was especially still. The day was
unusually balmy for the season, a mere half month since the vernal
equinox.

Were he not about to assassinate the Taka girl, he would have
enjoyed the morning by taking a stroll along the top of the bluffs.
But with two thousand pieces of gold still to earn, he had to remain vigilant. There would be plenty of time for enjoyment after
he disposed of her—short work to kill an inexperienced girl who
was but seventeen springs, almost two full years younger than he
had been when he killed his first man. With luck, Saburo would
head back to the Isle of Two Kingdoms before the sun reached
mid-heaven.

Saburo was infrequently called upon to kill women, and even
fewer times had he killed girls. However, he did not allow himself
to feel sorry for any of his targets. That sort of indulgence was

something a professional could never afford. If he wanted to be sentimental about anything, he would be sentimental about the morning. Sitting on the shadowy trail, he watched the gulls wheel overhead and listened to the soothing sound of the ocean, contemplating the beauty of the world, much as he had when he had manned the main gate at the monastery years before.

He again peered over the side of the bluff. Far below at the shore, he saw the white-and-orange robes of the two ninja disguised as monks. Saburo immediately grew annoyed. They were supposed to wait at the top of Carriage Road should Yamabuki take it down to the shore instead of Foot Trail. Already they had mishandled their mission. Saburo did not know the actual names of the two ninja, nor did he want to know, nor did he care. They boasted that together they had killed over twenty men. But they were young. Inexperienced.

His musings were interrupted by shouts and singing echoing off the cove's sheer walls. At water's edge, a *kobune* packed with Ōuchi samurai glided toward shore. Once they landed, chances were the warriors would come up Foot Trail, and a trail teeming with samurai would make it almost impossible to carry out a discreet assassination.

Saburo only hoped the Ōuchi would clear out by the time that Yamabuki appeared; otherwise it would be up to Kuma's two ninja to intercept her. He had to make sure it did not come to that.

Soon the kobune would head back across the Strait. If the Taka girl had been waiting at the trailhead, probably she was now on her way down.

His patron had described her: quite tall, she would be wearing full armor composed of dark-pine-green-lacquered *kozane* knotted together with cobalt-blue silk cords—a combination of weave and color typical of all Taka warriors. And she would travel without her personal bodyguards.

The first business for Saburo, however, was to deal with the disembarking Ōuchi, who had already come well up the trail. A lingering crabber who "just happened" to be standing around would be out of place and character.

Saburo pulled open the wicker door to the crab basket, shook the carrier hard, and about fifteen or so of the clawed creatures fell out. They immediately started to lumber along the dirt in the way of their kind. In a moment, he was on his knees with them.

"Shoo! Shoo!" he whispered, shoving the crabs along to get them moving. His head surreptitiously swiveling, Saburo waited, looking down the trail for the Ōuchi, and up the trail for his victim.

The Ōuchi appeared first. Saburo lifted his hands helplessly as they started to stream past him.

"Oh no," he moaned. "My catch! My catch! Oh please, Great Buddha, take pity on me."

The warriors, for their part, had enough room on the road to pass, for Saburo had staged his tragedy at the widest spot along the otherwise narrow trail. The Ōuchi continued on, some smirking at the crabber, others contemptuous in their feigned disinterest and nonchalance.

Every once in a while Saburo would pick up a crab, giving him a reason to slip his hand into the basket.

As the last of the forty or so Ōuchi headed on up the trail, out of the corner of his eye Saburo spied Yamabuki. The patron had described her perfectly, yet upon seeing her, there were a few critical details that had not been mentioned. For one, she led a massive battle horse. To fulfill the requirement of discreetly killing her, Saburo would have to deal with the mount after she was dead, and battle horses were temperamental and difficult to control. And this one would be conspicuous. Even more conspicuous would be a lowly crabber leading a mount of this kind. For the moment, he put it out of his mind. He would deal with the stallion when the time came. He had to kill Yamabuki first. He moved his hand toward the pike.

He expected someone thinner and shorter, but she was as tall as the tallest warriors. The armor blurred her sex. In full yoroi, and wearing a *kabuto*-style battle helmet that almost completely hid her face and hair, she easily could have been taken for a youth.

But the eyes. Oh, the eyes! Not the eager-to-please look, nor the haughtiness of some young, pampered aristocratic woman concerned more with looking appealing and seductive than paying attention to her surroundings, looking away, taunting men to pursue and by doing so, maybe winning favor.

This one's eyes met his directly. If Saburo looked too closely, he would give himself away, for no crabber would dare hold the eyes of a warrior. His eye patch helped him in this as he rolled his uncovered eye skyward, then flung himself to the ground in supplication, kowtowing as she approached.

Yamabuki came closer, holding the bridle with her right hand. Her tachi scabbard hung from her right hip.

Left-handed samurai.

She would draw from the side opposite from the one that he had expected. Saburo, groveling and chasing crabs, adjusted his position for a left-handed swordswoman, and slipped his hand into the basket. His fingers curled around the cold steel. With a soft, gentle pull, he loosened the weapon so it would move freely and easily when it was time to attack.

Yamabuki paused, yet she was not close enough.

She watched him. His hand had lingered in the basket perhaps too long. He removed his empty hand from the carrier, palms down. Feigning fear, not looking up but only at her waist, he eyed the spot in her corselet where his pike would break through with the least resistance.

He looked up to see where she was looking as he flashed a smile, expecting her to turn up her nose and look away like the Ōuchi had. But instead of moving on past him, she stood still.

"Eating crabs must bring you health," she said softly, touching her own mouth, apparently referring to his teeth, which were perfect. Too perfect for a crabber.

She began to lead the horse by its bridle around him. In two steps she would come so close he could touch her without moving. The basket was between them. He leaned toward it, continuing to eye the spot where he would bury the steel.

He was about to reach in when suddenly an enormous leg shot between Saburo and the basket. There was a crashing sound as the foot connected, sending the crab carrier flying at least ten lengths through the air, turning top over bottom before bouncing another few times far down the trail before rolling to a stop at a switchback.

Who dares!

SEVEN

AN INSTANT

I T IS SAID that for the Gods time passes differently. There is a story that has been handed down from one of the dynasties of the Yellow River:

A farmer, while walking over a windy mountain pass, happened upon two ancient-looking men who sat before a game board, playing *Wéi-Qí*. He paused for a moment to watch them make but a few moves of the black stones and white stones. Realizing it was impolite to stare, and having much to do, the farmer hastily moved on.

When the farmer arrived at his settlement, somehow everything seemed just a bit different. He quickly realized the settlement was filled with strangers. Where had they come from? He asked for his wife by name. He called each of his children's names aloud.

At last a very old woman, with the help of a walking stick, came out of one of the houses and drew close.

"Grandfather!" she gasped.

His misfortune was that he had stayed with the Immortals for what only seemed moments. For mortal man, sometimes life events flash by like lightning. At other times, moments stretch out like a long rain. It is how we experience the ever-changing changelessness of the universe.

Eight

Shima

W HEN SABURO HAD REACHED into the basket for the pike, it was the culmination of a long journey that was supposed to lead to the death of a comely young woman. A princess, at that. His fingers had been stretched out, not quite touching the steel. How unsettling it was when his weapon ended up out of reach, down the trail, as if the Gods had intervened!

A large warrior angrily stomped through the crabs, deliberately crushing them under foot.

Saburo almost dared not look up, for he knew who it was, yet he had no choice but to look long and hard.

Their eyes locked.

And in but one instant that felt like a lifetime, he indeed recognized the man. The warrior. His teacher. His friend.

Shima.

And even as the name rang in Saburo's ears, Shima's expression flashed at him as he marched by. Saburo could not name what he had seen. Yet he had seen all.

Despite years. Despite all that had happened—the camaraderie, struggles, love loss, disappointments, murders, and the ten years of stony separation—the two men instantly recognized that nothing had changed between them, both good and bad.

And yet at the same time, Shima looked completely different, even though in so many ways he had not changed at all. Shima had always taken great pride in his hair that flowed thick and black like a mane, but he had shaven both his beard and his head.

Was it even he? Of course it was. The eyes. The mouth. The stature. Bodies, even with years, do not change—at least not until they whither. This man's body was anything but withered. Saburo would never, and could never, forget Shima's. He remained tall and broad across the shoulders and obviously as strong as ever. Stronger, maybe, for he carried a *nodachi* over his shoulder. Too long to wear it across the hip, he shouldered the field sword in the manner of a spear.

In the next moment, Shima was gone.

Yamabuki, too, headed down Foot Trail, disappearing around a switchback. Getting away. But Saburo's only remaining weapon was the tantō he had in his sleeve—useless now.

Saburo leapt up, scrambled directly up the hill to a place in the line of sight of the beach. He unfurled a yellow silk scarf, the signal to the monks that he had not killed the Taka samurai. Moments later, a mirrored glint flashed back. They acknowledged. It was now up to them.

He waited for some time, and then saw the kobune slipping out of the cove under sail. The green of Yamabuki's armor was unmistakable. Her black colt was in a horse blind next to a merchant cart. The two white-and-orange-robed ninja sat near the bow. Shima sat at the stern near the *senchou*. The remaining passengers, six in bright-green tunics, and one in white, sat in the middle of the boat. Saburo looked further into the channel. Boats from the opposite shore approached.

But then the *ōgane* temple bells boomed out. All along the hill-sides, the bells of the various temples began to toll their warning.

Saburo turned and ran headlong toward the docks.

By the time he reached the shore below, several boats had hur-riedly landed.

A wave of new passengers wanted to cross, but instead of board-ing, they milled about. Saburo was told that with a storm coming in, the captains were loath to risk the channel until what the priests had seen from the hilltops blew through.

Saburo seethed. Yamabuki would make it to Honshu while he remained marooned on the southern isle. Once she started inland, finding her would become ever harder, and the longer he waited, the further inland she would go, with any number of roads, paths, and trails to take.

The air felt damp. Gulls riding air currents headed inland.

Saburo was not going anywhere. He looked skyward. Were the Gods laughing at him?

NINE

LEAVE NOW AND MAKE ALL SPEED

TETSU, A SHOUT BOAT'S senchou, sat completely relaxed on the gangway that led to a particularly sturdy-looking kobune. Saburo strode up to the captain, and without so much as an exchange of words, thrust something into the captain's hand.

The senchou looked at what he had been given. Six *kaiki shoho* rested in his calloused hand. A slight grin came to his lips. Silently he mouthed, *Gold.* His eyes shot up, and he carefully studied the simply dressed man who had just given him several times more money than Tetsu would have made in a good month.

Saburo muttered, "Leave *now.* Just me . . . and make all speed."

Tetsu casually turned his head to look west. The sky was darkening. He looked to the eastern horizon and the bright cloudless sea. The ōgane continued to toll. He slowly shook his head.

Saburo added quietly, "If you make extra speed, I'll double it . . . when we get there, that is."

"Hm," Tetsu sighed. Merely an advance for a half-hour dash across the Barrier Strait. Indeed, if they left now, they just might well get the boat across before the storm hit. Fingering the money, this time he nodded and almost absentmindedly slipped the gold into his sleeve pocket. Tetsu indicated the gangplank. Saburo boarded at once.

Tetsu then screwed his face into a scowl, almost bolting up, now glaring at the waiting crowd, and bellowed, "No room! Go elsewhere!"

A collective gasp arose from the passengers. He waved them away.

"We're casting off! We're heading out!"

The crew, also dumbfounded, looked at the senchou. Tetsu pointed to his own sleeve pocket, where he always kept passengers' payments, and nodded hard. He then gestured toward the incoming front.

The crew, getting his drift, immediately joined in, waving their arms as if they were chasing off flies. "Next boat! Go away! We're casting off! We're heading out!"

The other boatmen had seen nothing like it. They craned their necks as the lone passenger sat down near the bow of the shout. What could possibly motivate the senchou to take his craft across the Barrier when there was the possibility of a gale? A few of the most seasoned captains shook their heads. They had seen skies just like this before, and they murmured a prophecy: *Look long and hard, for we shall never see that boat or its crew again.*

TEN

THE MAN OF IRON

THE CROSSING STARTED OFF smoothly enough, but no sooner had the boat moved into the Strait's more open waters than the seas grew rough as intermittent gusts buffeted the craft. Almost at once, high clouds roiled over the far hills. It was only then that the boatmen fathomed what the priests saw from their hilltop temples.

Rapidly the blue western sky disappeared behind a thick cloak so dark that the west was almost night itself. Cold rain started to fall. As the wind picked up, it drove salty drizzle and spray ahead of it. If Tetsu harbored any doubts, he hid them down deep with the gold buried in his sleeve. In an almost brazen show of defiance, the captain now commanded his men to run up both of the shout's sails.

"Let's make speed. We have to be across before the storm hits," the senchou yelled to his men.

His crew, seemingly bolstered by their captain's confidence, pretended to be indifferent to the undulating sea as the shout picked up speed. It was the obvious thing to do: Outrun the incoming troughs. After all, far away, the Windward Sea in the east shone silvery and bright, almost placid. There *was* fair weather in the area if one only knew how to reach it.

Darkness quickly closed in overhead. The waters turned gray—all except the whitecaps that rose under a hard westerly wind.

"The sails are working against us!" the sail man cried out as he wrestled with the mast and cloth.

"We're getting nowhere!" the rope man strove to be heard over the sound of the waves.

"If we use *kyōfū* to blow us *down* the channel instead of fighting the crosswind, we'll have all the speed we can take!" the sail man shouted.

The senchou shoved the tiller over, hard, turning the boat toward the east.

ELEVEN

DRAGON'S THROAT

S ABURO'S STOMACH CHURNED. He lay against the hull, gripping the rail as the boat rode on into the narrow slot of ocean known as Dragon's Throat. Icy salt spray drenched him, though he shivered more from nausea than from the cold. Water came over the side as the boat began to broach.

From the sternpost tiller, Tetsu battled the waves, turning the boat sharply to prevent it from being swamped altogether. As it yawed, it listed heavily, teetering, now to starboard, now to port, as wave after wave rocked the kobune.

Tetsu cried orders to his crew. They sprang into action, and the haul-boat slowly but steadily started to come about until it headed in the same direction as the rollers that scuttled down through the Barrier Strait.

Each swell gently lifted the kobune's hull high and then slammed it down hard against the bottom of each trough, only to lift it up yet again, over and over, until Saburo's head spun and his gorge rose. Gagging on his own spew, he got to his feet and staggered further forward, where he bent his head over the side and unceremoniously retched into the waves. The spindrift spit into his face, stung his one exposed eye, and filled his half-open mouth with saltwater.

Saburo spat back and cursed. There was little doubt in his mind that Yamabuki was already on the opposite shore.

Tetsu barked, "Everyone! Tie in!"

His words were still hanging in the air as the crew nimbly strung and secured a heavy rope-line stem to stern, and then proceeded to tie cinch-ropes around their own waists, after which they hitched the free ends via slipknots to the trunk line. The crew exchanged looks when their sole passenger, who was dressed like a fisherman and was therefore assumed to know the ways of the sea, failed to likewise tie in.

The captain grew wroth, shook his finger at Saburo, and bellowed, "Him too!"

The deck man immediately made his way forward. Taken by surprise, Saburo struggled. He wanted no part of any rope. The line reminded him of his own vow: he would never be captured; he would never be taken alive. Resist as Saburo might, the deck man handily pulled the cinch-rope around him just before the crabber's footing gave way when a particularly heavy wave hit. Saburo tumbled, but now cinched, the security rope smartly snapped taut; he only fell against the hull instead of toppling over the side.

Getting to his knees and again hugging the rail, Saburo choked, "You're not sailing where I told you to."

The deck man growled, "Thank the *Gods* that the boat's still riding. Thank them you aren't with some second-rate shout-men." The deck man turned his back, leaving the crabber to his hopeless gagging. It was best to look away. Seasickness was an infection spread as much by sight and idea as by any roll or pitch of waves.

Saburo went back to heaving his gorge over the side, but by now there was none left in him. He gasped as his gut muscles cramped themselves into knots.

The view over the side only made his seasickness worse. One moment, the waters swelled into towering mounds overhead; the next, they fell away so that he found himself peering into an ocean gulley. The only thing that did not undulate was the kobune's wooden hull. Everything else constantly shifted shape, for such is the way of water: it's a changeling, whether a man looks out with two good eyes or wears an eye patch over one to disguise it.

He closed his uncovered eye to blank out the movement, yet he felt each rhythmic lurch. Still at one with the boat, in his mind he visualized how it bobbed and yawed with every roller.

My eye is closed, but I still "see."

He knew he needed to think of something other than the waves, otherwise the nausea would not stop. A master assassin, Saburo succeeded in his shadowy enterprises because he was almost always at one with his surroundings. However, now was not the time to reach outside with his senses. It was time to mute them. He gritted his teeth.

I am here by choice.

He could not let his anger with the sea and the state of his stomach determine what was in his head.

"Ahh!" the sail man screamed and pointed downwind. Further east in the channel, another boat heaved and yawed, waves foaming about its hull. This was one of the largest of the haul-boat types, a *fune*, loaded down with carts, goods, and at least eighty people.

The fune rocked side to side as roller after roller hit it broadside.

Bolts of lightning flashed, striking the ocean near the larger craft, momentarily leaving big circles of white light under the dark blue waters.

"Raijin is beating the heavenly drums!" cried the rope man.

"The Storm God's urging us to sail faster!" Tetsu bellowed.

A great peal of thunder rolled down the channel. Everything flashed white as a bolt of lightning struck the fune with a sound that broke the sky open, shattering the fune's bare mast. Fire and smoke leapt skyward as the mast toppled. Just then a large oncoming roller hit the fune, causing it to list even more heavily. Though the boat righted, it was obvious the vessel had taken on water and was now beginning to founder.

Frantic figures could be seen cutting carts loose, pushing them and any cargo overboard. The swell must have also swept some of the passengers overboard, for heads bobbed among waves. The crew of the fune extended long poles to pull the swimmers back aboard the stricken boat. The merchant carts floated free of the hull and swirled in the current. The swimmers who could not grab onto the poles clung to the debris, which itself began to sink. The fune took on more and more water until every wave washed over its sides.

The hull disappeared, and then the masts slipped beneath the waters.

The current and winds quickly took the shout past the remainder of the wreck. The people clinging to whatever floated cried out. The current continued to pull them away.

"Put out the poles! Haul them aboard!" the sail man shouted over the crash of the seas. "We must help them!"

"Yes! We must help," and "They'd do it for us," cried the others.

Saburo ominously lifted his head, staring at each of the shout's crew in turn. One would think that a common crabber with vomit across his face and with only one good eye would not inspire much in the way of command, but he set his jaw.

Pointing down the channel, the crabber growled, "No room. No time. Raijin has spoken. Would you challenge the God of Lightning Storms? Hide your belly buttons lest He come and tear your insides out."

The one-eyed man had spoken to the shout's crew as if they were mere children, invoking the childhood story of the Thunder God, who would take out a child's insides and eat them during a storm. Parents warned their children to cover their little bellies with their hands, lest Raijin feast on them.

But it was not Raijin that the sailors feared. Something passed between the one-eyed man and the four boatmen. Gone was the guise of the somewhat bumbling old crab fisherman, the hapless passenger green to the gills who hung over the side of the boat. That one eye shone with malevolence. That one eye bored into them in a way that took away whatever light was around them, like he was death itself. He wielded no sword. He raised no weapon. But at that moment they knew he was ready and capable of killing them all. And they realized that it did not matter to him, having killed them, that he would be left to fight the waves on his own. And though this was not Saburo's boat—he had merely hired it—they gave up any thought of trying to help the fune.

Later they would tell themselves that there was no hope. And they would be right. They also would console themselves that they likely would have lost their own boat and their own lives, and surely the handsome bonus the one-eyed man had promised them. There was nothing that they could have done. And they would have been right in that, too. At that moment, never questioning and never looking over their shoulders, the shout's crew turned east, setting off for Akamagaseki, the wind at their backs.

The wind drowned the faraway cries of the doomed. The last of the debris disappeared into the froth. There was nothing to see but angry water.

Twelve
AKAMAGASEKI

T HE KOBUNE GLIDED into the shallows of Akamagaseki in the midst of the icy rain but, save for the water she had taken on, outwardly the shout boat looked no worse for the wear. As promised, the one-eyed crabber handed the senchou six additional gold coins. Done with the boat and crew, the assassin turned his back and headed toward the hill-shore town.

Akamagaseki consisted of about a hundred buildings spread along the North Road which wound down out of the high hills. Saburo surveyed the town, looking for her distinctive mount, but it was nowhere to be seen. Yamabuki had long since passed through the town.

Saburo could not go after her with only a tantō and wearing a fisherman's tunic.

He saw a brown-and-white banner flying from a workshop proudly proclaiming *Katchū-shi:* armorer. Upon entry, Saburo saw assorted pieces of armor stacked everywhere.

The shop was unusually large for a town so small as Akamagaseki. Yet, for all the armor, no one was working on, fixing, or crafting new armor. And there was no forge.

This is no Katchū-shi's shop. A trader, not a craftsman.

A surly man in a tunic begrudgingly walked up to Saburo, eyeing him with disdain. Almost sneering, he said, "We don't need any *kani* here. Go sell your crabs elsewhere."

"I am not selling kani," said Saburo.

"Rain's stopped," the sour man said. "This is a shop. You can wait outside, or go to the inn to dry off."

"I am looking for armor."

The man cast a skeptical look. "Armor?"

Saburo nodded.

The shopkeeper hissed, "This is a top-class shop. I deal with samurai and even the *kuge*." The man again looked him up and down, and said, "There aren't enough crabs in a basket to buy even a frayed silk drawstring. Besides, I don't trade."

"I'm fresh out of crabs," Saburo said softly, his eyes wandering over the jumbled armor inside the shop.

"You have money, then?"

Saburo again nodded, already looking at the pieces that caught his fancy. Black. He liked black. It helped in the night.

The merchant's eyes darkened. Evidently he was calculating something. "What are you looking to buy?" he asked warily.

"What about that chest protector over there?" Saburo said, inclining his head toward one which bore the dark-red Hayakawa emblem, a mon with double-edged swords. The armor itself was composed of black iron platelets tied with black silk cords.

"Too expensive for you," the man grunted. "Three gold coins."

Saburo walked over and picked up the chest protector and raised it to his chest. "About the right fit."

The merchant stiffened and spoke formally. "It was sold to me by a man who needed to book passage across the Strait. He was very sad. His ancestral armor."

"*His* armor?" Saburo looked the shopkeeper directly in the eye. "Then why is there blood on the cords here?" He touched it near the shoulder.

The trader dismissed him with a wave. "Maybe some dirt is all."

"A 'top-class shop' with dirt on the armor?" Saburo put his nose to the discolored cords and made a face. "And it even *smells* of blood." He shook his head slowly.

The trader's eyes narrowed and he again looked the filthy crabber over with disdain.

Bluntly, Saburo said, "I think you did not buy this from its owner—at least not the one who wore it when the blood was spilled. I will hazard that the stains are the owner's blood, and you bought the armor from someone who stripped the dead."

The trader blanched and looked angry, upset, and frightened all at the same moment. "You—"

"But," Saburo said, cutting him off, "I do think this will do well for me." He stroked his chin whiskers slowly. "I will give you twenty-five pieces of silver for the *dō* and the rest of the armor that goes with it."

"I don't have any more parts . . ." the trader began, but before he could finish, Saburo fished out from the pile the shin, shoulder, and sleeve guards, along with all the rest of the accoutrements.

"Where's the kabuto?" Saburo asked.

The trader took a deep breath, as if unsure he wanted to divulge this information. But when Saburo started digging through a large box, the trader said, "The helmet did not fare so well."

Saburo pulled out the shattered kabuto. Indeed, whoever

delivered that blow had broken through iron. He turned a baleful eye to the man, who seemed to wither under the gaze. "Did you get any weapons with the trade of this particular yoroi?"

The man muttered, "A medium sword."

"No tachi?"

"I'm only an armorer."

Saburo snorted at the assertion.

The man put up his hands in appeal. "I don't get many weapons, and tachi usually get taken first thing."

"Show me the medium sword."

The man, still skeptical about this customer, produced a black scabbard. It, too, bore the sacred mon of the *ken*.

The trader stepped back, stifling a gasp, as Saburo grabbed the scabbard and pulled the medium sword out fully, holding it against the light of the brightening day. The blade edge was flawless.

The man's face dropped as the crab fisherman knocked out the pins on the tang and pulled the handle off the sword. "Ha!" Saburo exclaimed, immediately recognizing the name of the smith. "Kuninaga," he whispered. "I'll give you a piece of gold for all the armor if you throw in this sword."

"Hm!" the merchant gruffed, face sour.

But then Saburo pulled a *ryō* coin out of his sleeve and held it up so that the gold would catch the light, gleaming just as the sword had. Saburo's silent question was meant to vex the merchant: what was more valuable—steel or gold?

The man's eyes lingered on the coin. Then nodded hard.

Saburo slapped the coin into the merchant's hand. "Now where can I shave?"

THIRTEEN

A WELL-TRODDEN TRAIL

S ABURO HURRIEDLY SHAVED his beard and moustache, and trimmed his wild mane before rinsing away the remnants of the lampblack-and-lard compound that the morning's rains had not already washed out. Even after applying a "special oil" that he carried with him specifically for removing the coloring, his hair still held a dark, silver-gray cast instead of its natural pure white. Nevertheless, towel dried, oiled, and combed, his fresh hair gave him a distinguished look. Almost regal.

He emerged from the armor shop wearing the all-black yoroi with the well-sharpened personal sword in its black scabbard tucked into his sash. He had also obtained a set of straw boots, a straw rain cloak, and straw umbrella hat—the clothing of a traveling warrior—thrown in for another piece of silver.

He regretted that there were no riding horses available in Akamagaseki, but he did not regret taking the time to put on a new disguise. Only those with the most sensitive discernment would ever have suspected that he was the same man who, within the same hour, had entered the town, looking like a hapless, disheveled, and lowly crab fisherman.

He now blended in as a typical warrior on his way home to Sagami Prefecture, home of the Hayakawa, which was in the same direction that Yamabuki traveled. It helped that Saburo been to Sagami. It was what had first attracted him to the armor, for he knew enough of the province so that if he were questioned at any of the Prefecture crossings, he would have a solid story. A perfect guise to travel.

Also, with his hair back to its natural silver and his beard shaved, he looked nothing like the crabber he had made himself out to be that morning. And the eye patch. Always good! It's what people saw first and remembered the most, forgetting the details of the rest.

But for all his nobility, as Saburo headed along the street he had to step around an assortment of animal manure and human excrement piles typical of all cities and settlements—even in the capital. He casually tossed the tattered eye patch into one particularly fresh heap. The man was still tying his pants up as Saburo walked by.

Without the patch, Saburo's depth perception returned.

Yamabuki certainly would not recognize him now. But she had a significant head start. Hopefully, his two accomplices had already killed her. Nevertheless, he had to hurry.

He started walking at a brisk pace. Yes. It would all be good.

FOURTEEN

WE'LL BE IN KITA BY THE
HOUR OF THE SHEEP

OJI-SAN BLEW HIS breath out. It steamed. "Walk faster. It's starting to get colder." The old man cast a worried look at the old woman, then nodded encouragingly at the three young people that the elders led. "No good getting to the docks only to wave farewell. They're here to trade. But once they sail west, they won't be back for another year."

"Listen to Oji-san," Obā-san said solemnly. "We don't want to return without coins—just with five unsold baskets of cloth."

Sa-ye, along with her husband to be, Maho, and her older brother, Karasu, followed behind old Oji-san and old Obā-san, who knew the way to the southern-most isle. The two gray elders had made the trip since *their* grandparents led *them*.

"Hah!" Oji-san grunted confidently. "We're close to the Strait. Can you smell the sea?"

Sa-ye took a deep breath and smiled in return. "Yes."

"You of all people should know the sea smell," said Obā-san. "Your mother gave birth to you on a fishing skiff."

Sa-ye laughed at the familiar story, adding, "and then went right back to diving for *awabi* while the boat rocked me." Everyone laughed. It was a good story.

Oji-san said, "Your nose sometimes helps more on the trail than your eyes. If the Gods favor us, we'll soon be at the channel and in Kita by the Hour of the Sheep."

All five walked slightly stooped over to better heft the covered baskets slung across their backs.

Carrying walking sticks that could double as makeshift spears, the two young men had been told by their settlement's headman to escort the others. Besides being of help to the two elders, Maho was glad to come along, for it also meant that instead of working in the fields he could spend four days, in each direction, talking with Sa-ye—something he enjoyed above all else.

As for Karasu, he wanted to see the strange foreign people and their giant ships. Now there would be stories to tell for the rest of his days. He had never been more than a day's walk from Home Settlement.

In fact, none of the younger ones had been this far from home. Today would be one of great excitement. They would hire a boat and sail across the famous Barrier Strait to the Isle of Unknown Fires.

Oji-san cleared his throat. "We'll need to get a good boat captain, but one we can afford. The bigger haul boats, like the *mifune*, are for carts, horses, and cargo. All we need to carry is ourselves and our packs, so a kobune, or even a shout boat, will be enough." He added with a whisper, "And cheaper. Let me do the talking with the senchou. I've met a few of them and I remember those who are good boat captains, and I remember the cheats."

"It's midday, but it's getting darker," said Maho.

Thunder rolled through the forest. Hail started to fall. "You think the Gods are sending us a warning?" Sa-ye asked.

"We can't let the cloth get wet!" Karasu cried.

Everyone broke into a run. Rounding a bend they saw a cliff with a natural overhang. It was large enough for them and their five packs. The hail fell rapidly as the farmers scurried under the shelter.

"Huddle together," Obā-san instructed. "Stay warm."

The hail fell harder yet, but beneath the outcropped cliff they were dry.

"You think it still might snow?" Sa-ye asked.

"Such a strange storm," said Maho.

The hail finally turned to rain before coming to a stop. Silence fell over the forest.

"I did not think it could be so loud," said Karasu.

The five farmers got up off the dirt and brushed their bottoms. Obā-san said, "Turn. Brush the hail off your baskets, too."

"Yes!" Oji-san cackled. "Yes. Listen to Obā-san."

Turning their backs, they went to clearing hail and rain from one another's packs.

The clouds began to break and the sky turned blue. The sun shone on the ice pebbles.

"It's so beautiful," said Sa-ye, looking up and down the forest road.

"You sound like you've never seen hail before," Maho laughed.

"The ground's covered with pearls," Sa-ye said. "It's like the Sea Goddess dropped them to remind us of home."

"You think the oddest things, Sa-ye," Maho teased, obviously delighted by everything she said.

"You've got to agree with Sa-ye, though. It's pretty," said Karasu.

Maho sniffed and wiped his nose with his sleeve to push back the chill.

"Ha!" Oji-san snorted to see if his breath steamed. "See? Not so cold. It'll warm up soon." Everyone listened respectfully. "Back when I was a boy, the summers were hotter and the winters warmer. Now? The summers are cooler and the winters are longer." Oji-san scowled. "Colder these days."

"Cold," Obā-san repeated, nodding her agreement.

Karasu and Maho smirked.

"Don't be so sure of yourselves," Obā-san chided. "You boys think, like I did when I was your age, that every elder feels the cold more with every year." She sniffed. "And maybe we do, but I also remember like yesterday that the cherries blossomed by the first day of spring. Now it's always later than that." She turned away.

"Forests and fields change with time, like the color of hair." Oji-san ran his palm across his face. "But cliffs and hills are slow to change. Study them and learn the land's face so that when we go home, or you come back some other time, leading youngsters of your own . . ." he said, laughing and pointing at Sa-ye's belly.

Maho laughed. Sa-ye giggled and blushed.

Oji-san continued, ". . . you'll recognize the land like an old friend. Remember how the road looks over your shoulder. It'll be the face it shows us on our way back. Did I tell you that?"

"You've told them. I've told them." Obā-san sniggered. "We should make *them* tell *us*, like the old ones made *us* do when we were young."

Oji-san said, "Let's all sing. It's downhill all the way to the shore."

All five broke into broad smiles of anticipation and let their song fill the noonday as they quickly picked up their pace:

The road is high,
The road is low,
Let the road rise and fall,
Our loads are light,
Carry, carry,
We will get there,
Journey on with smiles and song.

"I remember this bend," Oji-san said, pointing toward a high clay cliff on one side of the road and a steep drop-off on the other. "There's a Shintō shrine there. We're almost at Akamagaseki now." He rubbed his hands together. "Let's keep singing so the shrine God hears us coming and is pleased."

They continued in song, smiling and singing with a spring in their steps. But as they rounded the bend, the five stopped in their tracks and fell totally quiet.

A samurai, sword high, blocked the road.

Sa-ye gasped. *A woman samurai?*

Sa-ye had trouble making sense of what her eyes were showing her: a woman with long, long hair, but wearing armor. It was this very strangeness that kept her from becoming terrified. She looked to the others. Maybe they could explain what they had come upon, but they did not exchange glances with Sa-ye. Instead, like four ashen statues, they stood frozen, their unblinking eyes fixed on the warrior holding a drawn sword.

The warrior's back was to them, and her sword was pointed away. She seemed lost in thought, gazing into the blade's edge.

Three men lay at her feet, perfectly still, as if they were asleep. *Why are they on the ground when it's so wet?*

The warrior stood next to a jet-black horse. Like the samurai, it was geared for battle, bedecked with dark-red braid, cords, tassels, and lacing. A sword-tipped lance, attached to the tack through a series of leather straps, poked upright into the sky. A quiver brimming with arrows hung down just behind the saddle. A bow was attached next to it. The warrior's helmet rested on the saddle pommel.

A glint of light flashed off the blade edge and into Sa-ye's eyes.

The warrior turned on her heel, smartly, but without seeming to be startled. She did not brandish the weapon. She merely stood there, looking at them in puzzlement, then lowered the sword to her side.

Sa-ye breathed a bit more easily.

The warrior's armor was colorful—cobalt-blue silk interlacing dark-green-lacquered iron platelets. This was not just an ordinary warrior. What warrior could be called "ordinary"? This one was very wealthy. In fact, Sa-ye suspected that the warrior was someone highborn. Only a noblewoman would have hair that fell past her waist. She had tied it with dark-green ribbons that looked striking against her tresses as black as her colt. Like all nobles, she was beautiful. Her features were fair and free, though a fresh gash marred her cheek. The armor, too, was gashed just below the warrior's breasts.

Though Sa-ye knew little of weapons and swords—just enough to know to stay away from the people who carried them—she knew cloth and silk. After all, they carried colorfully dyed cloth and silk in the baskets on their backs.

Even at this distance, Sa-ye realized the warrior's split riding-skirt was a man's cut—blanched rough-hewn silk with some sort of pale-green print pattern. Such a *hakama* would cost an ordinary farmer five year's earnings—maybe even more. And though it was beautifully made, the riding-skirt was mud spattered. Sa-ye looked closer. *Blood.* And not just on the split-skirt, but on the woman's armor as well. The dark-green color had hidden the stains, but once she recognized what it was, Sa-ye saw that it covered everything, including the samurai's blade.

It was then that she allowed herself to look closer at the three "sleeping" men. They were even more bloody than the woman. They were dead.

Sa-ye suddenly couldn't breathe. "Oji-san," she moaned.

"Say nothing," Obā-san whispered.

"Give no offense," Oji-san muttered.

How could she give offense? They had done nothing to the samurai. The farmers were merely walking along the road. What offense was there in that? And yet the warrior stood over three dead bodies. The noblewoman, for all her beauty, status, and wealth, was a killer if she was nothing else.

With growing dread, Sa-ye recalled tales told at Home Settlement. It was said that there were those who committed skill-testing murders for the pleasure of it. She had only half believed, thinking that the stories were repeated on hot nights to send chills down everyone's backs.

Two of the dead were Buddhist monks. Did they give offense? How could they be a threat to anyone? Hardly more than beggars with holiness in their eyes.

"Oh mother," she stammered. She felt her knees grow weak.

"Brace up," Oji-san muttered.

"Hai!" she whispered with resolve, but then realized Oji-san was addressing Maho, who, unable to stand, had started to lean on the old man.

Suddenly the samurai raised her free arm over her head. Her voice filled the clearing. "Calm yourselves!" It was a young woman's voice—a strange accent—though she spoke in the manner of commoners. "These men are brigands!" The warrior swept her blade downward as though it were part of her hand, pointing in the direction of the dead as if there might be some confusion about whom she spoke. She then used lofty High Court words: "These miscreants were pretending to be what they were not."

Sa-ye could not quite follow.

Oji-san muttered. "I think she's saying those are robbers in disguise."

"It is good I happened along," the warrior said calmly. "With types such as these, there is no telling what they might have done had they found you first. Those two?" The samurai indicated the monks. "Assassins who kill for money." The warrior pointed her sword at the large dead man in armor. "Him?" The noblewoman looked directly at Sa-ye, exchanging a look that women share when they wish to convey a special meaning to another. "I carry a sword, and yet he tried to force himself. He wanted to have his way with me."

She held Sa-ye's gaze for a moment, then sheathed her sword.

FIFTEEN

YOU WILL DIE IN MOMENTS

MOCHIZUKI SNORTED NERVOUSLY, but with ease Yamabuki calmed the colt, then in one motion swung up into the saddle. She grew thoughtful. "I would not touch those bodies," she said to the farmers. "The monks tipped their blades with *fugu* poison. If it gets on you, you will die in moments. Not pretty."

Yamabuki could see that these farmers wanted nothing to do with any of the dead, or her. Good.

"Grandfather," she said. "Can you tell me where this road leads?"

"Hai," the older farmer said nervously. "It goes to Nagato."

"Is it the way to the Pass of the Setting Sun?" she asked.

He nodded.

"Any towns before I get to the pass?"

The old man hesitated, as if trying to think. "Minezaki," he said at last.

"Peninsula Ridge," she repeated, and pointed at the break in her armor. "Is there an armorer there?"

The farmers looked at each other. Finally the old man said, "I've never needed an armorer."

Yamabuki scowled. "Did I ask you if *you* needed an armorer?

Isn't it obvious that it is I who is in need?" she said, tapping the corselet.

As one, all five of the farmers bowed, trembling.

"I am not looking for your obedience. Answer me, or say you don't know!"

"Hai!" the old man's voice creaked. "They did, last time I heard."

"And how long ago was last time?"

"Ah?" The old man looked worried.

Now it seemed it was old woman's turn to speak. "We don't know. We've never been there. They say there's some fancy armorer from the capital there. We don't go there. Bad town. There's a war going on. Best stay away."

"Any other towns between there and the pass?"

"No," said the old woman. "Minezaki's the last town. The road goes up to the summit. Once you're on it, they say you either go through the mountains or turn back."

Yamabuki grinned. "Thank you for the advice, Grandmother." She nodded to them—they were excused. They could leave. They could move on.

Yet they did not move. They stood mute, the heavy loads strapped to their shoulders giving them the appearance of humpbacks. What strength these farmers had! It was obvious in their naked calves. Even the girl had the legs of a soldier.

Back at the Taka compound, no female, except a woman warrior, had anything but spindly legs. Lithe limbs. All of which said that women of nobility never worked in any real capacity, except to bear the young.

Maybe it was as they said: their one duty was to make sure the lineage continued.

Giving a final nod to the farmers, Yamabuki wheeled her mount about and rode off.

The farmers looked at each other, and then at the dead.

"Move. Move," said the elders, pushing the young ones forward down the trail. "Nothing for us here."

As they headed down the hill, another squall blew in from the sea. The heavy rains returned.

Sixteen

Calligraphy Lesson

R AISED IN THE HOUSEHOLD of a warlord father, Yamabuki's earliest memories were of warriors. She was surrounded by them. Though she was always under the watchful eyes of her nursemaids and bodyguards, Yamabuki was accustomed to continual activities involving swords, bow and arrow, and feats of horsemanship.

When she could first hold a bamboo rod, her father's retainers taught her to wield it as a sword. Sometimes as a spear. Her small hands grew familiar with how to tightly grip the shaft without at the same time tightening her arms too much or locking the rest of her body. She learned to stay fluid.

Around the same time, she was taught to read and write. And when she held a calligraphy brush, she likewise held it firmly, yet moved it gracefully. Almost without effort.

The girl of barely four springs copied the first pictograms of the things that were around her, and one of the first *kanji* she drew was a simple one: three strokes for *bushi*.

After a while, her tutor in all things, Nakagawa, pointed out that she was not being careful when she drew the pictogram for "warrior." At times, it looked like she made the symbol for "soil" because the lines were not precisely the right lengths. "Kouma," he said to her, "your father's retainers might not like being compared to 'soil.'"

He laughed, but she did not join in. It offended her young sensibilities that the people of the Yellow River Delta could not make the two calligraphies sufficiently different to tell soil apart from warrior.

Not long after, she learned to refine her strokes so that she could unambiguously distinguish between bushi

and *tsuchi*.

Yet it still bothered her.

What did the soil have to do with warriors?

SEVENTEEN

KARMA AND DUTY

YAMABUKI RODE FOR some time up the mountain highway toward the Pass of the Setting Sun. She looked behind, hoping from this elevation to glimpse the Isle of Unknown Fires across the faraway Strait, but storm clouds crept through the valley below, shrouding everything.

Although she was alone on the road, everywhere the terraced fields swarmed with farmers at work. She pulled back Mochizuki's reins. He snorted to a stop. She patted his mane, letting him rest and drink from a clear water rill. The trickle fed one of the rice basins near the road. Between lapping the water, he proceeded to rip a few tender green grasses that had sprung up near the runoff.

"Not much is it? Sorry." Though Mochizuki was well fed while stabled at the Wakatake Inn, she had been wise to also feed him just before crossing the Strait, and once again after they arrived in Akamagaseki. They were on the move and he was always hungry. His teeth tore at the meagre shoots. His chewing started her stomach to growl. She unstoppered her bamboo canteen and drained down the last of her saké.

Looking out across the rice basins, the day's events ran through her mind. She was hardly more than ten days from home and she had killed. Men had died.

It still did not seem completely real. Yet nothing could be more real: The fresh cut to her cheek that still oozed blood. The gash across her corselet. The fencing master's blood spattered all over her. Her scored blade edge.

Is this what being a warrior means?

But it was exactly as her mother had prophesized. She was alone in her thoughts and had no one to talk to about the emotional cost of killing.

She watched the farmers going about their work, oblivious to her. She might as well have been a cloud drifting by. No matter what happened, the farmers always worked on, through floods, droughts, blight, heat, and cold. Like soldiers, they did what it was given to them to do.

Back down the road, the five traveling farmers certainly had not asked what had led up to the duel. All they wanted was to get away. What happened in the day-to-day lives of the *buké* did not matter to them.

Likewise, the rulers did not care about the farmers so long as the rice crop was plentiful and the rice tax was paid.

The farmers worked the dried-mud basins, which had not been touched since last year's harvest. They beat the hardpan with staves, turning the drudgery into a celebration called *ta no kami matsuri*, the rite of soil breaking. The goal was to re-soften the earth to make it ready for re-flooding, to be followed by the planting of young rice shoots, just in time for the Plum Rains hardly a month away.

The farmers meticulously pounded the caked clumps of dirt,

their staves striking the soil to a rhythm that merged into a collective *thub-thub-thub* pulse.

"Hear that, Mochizuki?" She smiled. "Even when they pound the dirt, they turn it into music."

And though most of the farmers were working the soil within the shadow of levee walls, some placed large sunflower stalks bundled together, standing as tall as a man, to guard each field corner. Others danced on top of the embankments. Hands moving. Imploring. She clearly heard the words of their song sung in the local midlander dialect. Would that the Gods of Harm and Misfortune please move on to plague some other fields! Some other settlement! Some other place. Please, bad luck, go to another place to bring woe!

Then the melody changed. The thumping mixed with voices of a melancholy workers' song—happy, yet with an air of lament borne out of resignation.

Rise and rise and rise and fall,
Do not cry,
The mountains surround us,
The sun ascends,
As we toil at the soil.

Dance and dance and dance and fall,
Carry your crying child to bed,
Are the stars fireflies,
The gleaming tears at night-fall?
Hush now for tomorrow we rise to toil yet again.

The song was strangely soothing. And though the singers were but commoners, Yamabuki was swept up in its spell. She grasped that she shared karma with them—with all living things. As the song suggested, one's work was something that had to be endured until destiny ran its course. Swinging a stave, swinging a sword, it was all the same: theirs as workers of the soil, hers as a bushi. The things of life were not just done once.

Indeed, her travails were not over, at least not if she heeded the fencing master's words. Before their blades ever crossed, he said there would be more ninja. Maybe he was merely trying to unnerve her, but he predicted they would keep coming until they had the dispatches she carried.

Strange.

They kept talking about two scrolls when in fact she carried three. How was it that they did not know about the third scroll? And which one was the *third* scroll?

She shook her head, feeling dazed—she supposed, in part, because the wine had gone straight to her head. She did not like it that her senses were affected.

If there are other assassins, I have to keep my head clear.

She had only eaten a handful of cold *mochi gome* since arriving on the Main Isle. The sticky, cold rice in Akamagaseki and the five oysters prior to boarding the shout boat were all she had eaten since leaving the Wakatake Inn. Not all that much. She should have eaten more that morning, but prior to the crossing she had been too excited to have much of an appetite.

Innkeeper Inu had prepared some raw *buri* preserved in rice, likely the last fish she would taste for some time. She dug into her saddlebag, where she found the yellowtail. Inu had pressed the morsel into her hand as she had mounted up to leave, and said to her, "Your favorite," and suggested she save it for an evening celebration after her first day on the Main Isle. She would not wait until evening.

I'm still alive. That's worth celebrating.

As she began to chew, the taste told her that the fish was already going bad. It was marginal at best, but she needed to clear her head and needed the food to overcome her dizziness. She forced it down.

She looked at the distant mountain range. She was headed inland and any fish she would eat there would make what she just ate seem like a delicacy.

She estimated Heian-kyō lay another eighteen days ahead. She was already two days ahead of schedule. If she cut another two days off this part of the journey, she would arrive at the Taka Palace just that much sooner with the dispatches.

She always carried them either in her saddlebag or on her person. And last night, when Ryuma came to her bedchamber, the scrolls were just in reach, same as her sword. Certainly Ryuma and she had other things on their minds in the darkness of the chamber.

But there had been an odd occurrence just prior to that which Yamabuki had dismissed at the time, but which no longer seemed so random: A man traveling by kago arrived long after dark, though she could not see him clearly from her window. The kago carriers practically demanded that they be allowed to enter the inn. Inu had told them the inn was full for the night. Only after Ryuma all but dismissed them in his manly samurai voice did the kago and its passenger depart.

Who was this stranger who demanded entrance? What did he really want? Was he the man that the fencing master had referred to as the master assassin? Was this the same man who went by the name Saburo?

Waiting by the roadside, speculating, would not bring her any answers. Minezaki lay at the end of this road. If she hurried, she could make the town before the sun set.

She was a samurai. If there were more assassins, she would deal with them, just as she had done earlier.

She urged Mochizuki forward to whatever unique karma she as a warrior was destined.

EIGHTEEN

GHOST TOWN

"WE MIGHT BE AT Minezaki," Yamabuki whispered to Mochizuki. She could not exactly be sure. Someone had made off with the town sign.

I suppose whoever took the sign needed it for firewood.

Commoners were a strange lot.

If anyone in this town were asked about the missing sign, the townspeople would say that robbers had taken it during the night and that the law should do something about it. They would complain loudly of the stream of dubious travelers passing through. If asked why the sign had not been replaced, the townspeople would say they couldn't read, let alone write, so how could they possibly be expected to make a new one? Besides, the people who lived there already knew the name of their town. All any stranger had to do was ask.

She looked up and down the street. There was no one to ask. Twenty or so ramshackle board buildings lined each side of the North Road. Narrow paths ran between the various run-down hovels that likely served as houses. Clusters of outbuildings and some additional structures stood behind most of the dwellings.

Yamabuki estimated that the town could shelter two hundred people, though none were in evidence.

Is this a ghost town?

But then she detected movement in some of the doorways.

She slipped her hand toward her right hip, resting her fingers against the leather and silk that wrapped her sword hilt.

Hunched figures lurked in the shade of rickety wooden overhanging roofs. The late-afternoon light revealed they were ordinary farmers. Maybe a weaver or peddler or two in their number, it was hard to tell. Unlike the aristocracy, where the type of kimono, hat, or crown immediately revealed a person's rank, standing, trade, or skill, and thus their role in society, commoners dressed pretty much the same.

Why are they so cautious? They afraid of me?

Lady Taka had counseled: "If others find out that you're a warlord's daughter, then ride proudly." Though that approach could invite its own sort of trouble, there was something in majesty that kept riff-raff away.

Spurring her mount, she let him carry her forward at an easy lope. Mochizuki always looked stately, at least that is what she thought. Wherever she rode, he made a good show. Why hold back now? The ninja already knew who she was.

As she rode into the town, she saw that the only semblance of prosperity was at a lackluster marketplace where a lone farmer stood before his cart of unsold winter wheat. Riding on by the dwellings, she studied the inhabitants. They, in turn, watched her without exactly staring. Every one of them was gray, stooped, and skeletal.

What's this place? The Land of Ancients? Everyone's at least fifty years old.

A man with white, thinning, disheveled hair sat on the crumbling remains of a rotted stump outside of a shack. She reined Mochizuki.

"Is this Minezaki?" she asked.

He grimaced toothlessly and feebly pointed to his ear.

Perhaps he could read lips. "Minezaki?" she repeated, mouthing her words broadly. He continued staring blankly.

She noticed an old woman standing in a nearby doorway. "Minezaki?" Yamabuki asked.

The crone cringed as if Yamabuki was about to beat her. Another man, one with resentful eyes, grabbed the woman's wrist and pulled her inside the house. Yamabuki grew annoyed as she watched the door being shoved shut with a bang and heard the barring timber being put into place.

"Slam it any harder and your hovel will fall in on itself," she muttered.

She shifted her weight in the swan-like stirrups. Her red oak saddle moaned as if expressing Yamabuki's growing frustration. She knew it wasn't easy for commoners to decipher her upper-class manner of speech, nor would their midlander ears make much sense of her attempt at the commoner's dialect.

She called out, "Is this Minezaki?"

She was met with only silence.

"A town of mutes!" she huffed and wheeled Mochizuki about. *I'd have a better chance conversing with oxen.*

Just then she spotted a strong-looking boy scurrying toward a passage between two buildings. The boy, almost a man, though not quite, wore a blue-gray tunic. His arms and legs protruded from the ragged, undersized garment.

Seeing her, he immediately picked up his pace, moving away though not exactly breaking into a run.

She pushed Mochizuki to a canter. In four easy strides, the horse was next to the youth. Mochizuki towered over the boy and in the saddle she loomed even higher. The boy stopped, frozen.

"You live here?" she asked.

Keeping eyes down, he nodded.

"Is this Minezaki?"

"Hai," he said at last, still looking down.

She breathed a small sigh of relief. "Finally . . . You the town headman?"

"No," he mumbled.

"I thought you might be. You're the only one I've met so far in this pathetic place who seems to know where he is."

He turned his head away.

"Look at me when I speak to you!"

He looked up and straight at her.

She wondered if he had his wits. Why would a perfectly fit-looking boy not be in the fields during the day? *What's wrong with him? Is he the town blockhead?*

Whether he was a fool or not, she did not have the time to look for yet someone else to question. This oaf would have to do. After all, he seemed capable of conversing. "Does this town have a Katchū-shi?" she asked.

"Hai!"

Yamabuki let a smile slip. "And what's the armor maker's name?"

"Kōno." The boy bowed quickly. He smiled at her, mirroring her mood.

"Kōno?" She shrugged. "Never heard of him," she sniffed, "Does this Kōno, or whatever his name is, know what he's doing or is he just some local, bumbling 'box maker'?" That is, a maker and mender of kettles and sundries.

The boy paused, probably not quite knowing how to answer, for if in the eyes of the samurai what he said proved wrong, for his "lie" she could beat him, or worse.

Sensing his predicament, she asked, "Do many people come to Kōno's armory?"

"Hai." The boy brightened up again. "Many. Everyone."

Everyone? Humph. Merely people this boy knows.

"Where's his shop?"

"On the Ledge."

"The Ledge?"

"Hai! Ledge Road." He turned and pointed down a faraway lane that branched off the main road and disappeared into the trees, close to the vertical cliffs that loomed over the town.

Yamabuki flicked her hand to dismiss the boy. She wheeled about and headed toward the yet-to-be-seen armory.

Mochizuki had taken no more than a few steps when she sensed a sudden movement out of the corner of her eyes. Instinctively she shot a look back over her shoulder only to catch a glimpse of movement between two buildings: the boy, at a full run, shouting something she could not hear.

NINETEEN

THE YOUNG WARLORD

E VEN IF IT WERE already twilight, which it was not quite yet, the boy would have known by habit where to dodge to avoid boulders, and where to weave so as not to take a misstep. Though not the fastest route, it skirted around small fences and bypassed fierce dogs. "She's here! She's here!" he shouted as he ran.

He arrived at a building flying tall, red banner flags. Breathless, he almost leapt to its main door, abruptly stopped, and rapped firmly.

"She's here! She's here!" He did not need to yell so loudly, for his voice already pierced the walls.

"Who's here?" demanded a resonant voice from inside. The weathered wooden door abruptly slid open.

Had it been Yamabuki who ran to the door, and not the boy, she would have described the man inside as young—about her years. Not yet able to sprout a beard, it made him handsome in a boyish way. He was old enough to have a full mane of hair that fell past his waist, which he had tied in a man's light-blue hair ribbon. He was as tall as Yamabuki. Slender yet muscular. The body of a natural swordsman. He had twinkling eyes that secreted mischief. If

Tomoko had a dashing older brother, this could well have been him.

But all this was lost on the boy who stood outside. What the boy saw and noticed, instead, was a well-built and regally dressed older man who spoke with a melodious baritone voice that gave him an air of authority, a reputed young warlord who traveled without his guards.

"The woman samurai. She just rode in! Riding a battle horse, just like a *tai-shōgun*," said the boy.

"Like a tai-shōgun? Fair of face?" the young warlord asked as he stepped onto the small outer porch.

"Beautiful. Just like you said. And she's been in battle. Her armor's bloody and she's been cut. Here." The boy drummed his fingers on his own cheek at the spot.

"Wounded?"

"I think a scratch. She's spattered in blood, but it's not hers . . . and she's angry. I think it's because her armor was damaged. It's torn," said the boy as he drew his finger in a line across his own breast.

"What color armor?"

"Dark green."

"Green?" The warlord seemed startled.

"Dark as mountain hardstone."

"What color mount?"

"Black."

The warlord's eyes narrowed.

"Black with a white blaze. Here." The boy moved his finger in a circle on his own forehead. "The rest is all black, right down to the hooves."

"Does she fly a clan banner?"

The boy stretched both hands out, making an "X" pattern with his fingers. "Feathers. Like this."

"Where's she now?"

"She's gone to Kōno's to fix her armor. She was angry, but when I said Kōno fixed armor, she was happy."

"Well. I think I shall have to pay my friend Kōno a visit." The warlord paused. "In the meantime, keep on the lookout for *another* woman samurai. She's fair. Exceedingly fair. She'll be riding a *dapple* horse. She'll be clad in bright-*red* armor with leaf-green cords." He paused. "You know the sign of the three-spoke pin-wheel?"

The boy nodded.

"Especially look for that sign. And if you happen to again see this other warrior—Broken Armor, is it?—come find me, even if it's late. Maybe she'll come to your father's establishment later."

The young warlord tossed the boy a copper, stepped back inside, and closed the door behind him.

The boy, delighting in the coin, walked away. He of course knew better than to reveal it to his father. His father would only take it.

He walked back onto the street as the light faded. He would keep his eyes open for another woman warrior. This one with the sign: *tomoe.*

TWENTY

A WARNING

Riding toward the armorer's, Yamabuki noticed two young women. They stood near the front of a building that flew a rustic, dark-green banner with a calligraphy,

酒

which even the illiterate could read: saké.

Both women held three-stringed musical instruments, some sort of local versions of the *samisen*. They hummed as they plucked out an unfamiliar tune.

There's no one nearby. Who are they playing for?

The women appeared quite pretty, wearing the tunics of the Ancient Religion, the Jingi Faith, whose female practitioners were fast fading away. The two women had taken the time to brush their hair and tie their tresses with colorful ribbons which peeked from bright, hood-like scarves that were draped over their shoulders. They wore leggings and half cloaks made of bear fur, like the people of the Barbarian Isle.

The two women looked up from their music and beamed.

They are wearing make-up. Entertainers in a town as small as this? How can they make a living just by singing?

As Yamabuki rode closer, she realized exactly how the two women made their living. They were *yahochi*. Though carefully costumed, the cut of their upper bodices revealed more womanliness than any holy woman would allow herself. Shamanesses fallen on hard times, they would smile and sing to help men pass the night. What better place to ply their trade than where lonely men flocked to grow drunk, happy, and brave?

She saw from their surprise that only now did the two women grasp that the samurai was female. One of the two entertainers, with flagging interest, looked away. It was unlikely that a female warrior would want to share a bed with either of the young women. Nevertheless, the other of the two continued smiling, holding Yamabuki's eyes for just a bit longer. Perhaps for her it did not matter whether a patron was a woman, so long as there was money to be made. She might even have had *that leaning*. But when the second girl finally noticed Yamabuki's bleeding cheek, torn armor, and blood-spattered riding-skirt, she instantly lowered her gaze and turned her head toward the strings of the samisen, mimicking that she had returned to rehearsing. However, though she plucked the strings, she no longer hummed.

"Ledge Road?" Yamabuki asked.

The second woman suddenly looked back up and stammered, "A cursed road. You're in danger." She looked back down. "You'll meet the undead."

Without another word, the two women hurried into the saké establishment.

Yamabuki rode on, releasing her own thoughts of carnal love to purge the darkness the shamaness had untethered. Yamabuki's thoughts wandered back to the Inn of Young Bamboo the previous evening. She pictured herself in the bedchamber, Ryuma's body over hers, his arms enfolding her. The throes of passion. She could almost smell the room, and definitely she recalled Ryuma's scent for it still lingered on her, but so then, too, did the smell of blood from this morning's combat.

Had the yahochi been able to smell it too? Perhaps.

She ran two naked fingers across her cheek. The gash still smarted, but at least it had finally stopped bleeding. It only oozed now. She wiped her fingertips clean by running them over her riding-skirt, leaving blots of whatever that pale liquid was that trickled from healing cuts.

Dirty weather had started to wander into the higher mountains, pushing dark clouds whose color usually portended snow. If it snowed, she could find herself more or less marooned for days in some shack waiting for the weather to clear—an easy mark for assassins. She of course could skirt the pass and take the coastal road, but that route added six days. Even more opportunity for the assassins.

There were those who might have advised Yamabuki to lay out charms and burn special herbs while chanting prayers for good weather.

Yamabuki took in a deep breath. *No!* The snows would come whether she chanted or not. Whatever would happen, would happen. As for the undead, they were no threat compared to the living—that she had learned this very day. The dead merely lay there. They were no threat once they had fallen.

Forgetting any warnings, she rode on toward the armory.

Twenty-One

The Girl

CROWS GLIDED OVERHEAD, cawing, swooping toward one another, fighting over something while Yamabuki followed the narrow road, which ran along a precipice on one side, a cliff on the other. Several tall buildings lay at the end of the road.

Reining Mochizuki, Yamabuki swung her foot over the saddle and leapt down onto dry ground—the day's earlier torrential rains had not so much as touched Minezaki.

She landed well enough, considering the weight of her armor. Gathering herself, she smiled at the irony of wearing something so heavy. If she had chosen to remain a Taka court-maiden, she would now be wearing twelve heavy kimono. The armor's bulk and weight, if anything, were less than the kimono's, or so she told herself.

As she reached up to take Mochizuki's bridle, out of the corner of her eye she noticed a small girl of not more than four springs. All by herself, the child stood in the middle of the road up ahead, within the dark shadow of the high bluffs.

The girl looked down at an indentation in the dirt, and then looked up, gazing first at the warrior and then the battle horse.

Satisfying whatever curiosity she might have had, the girl looked back down and started to pound the ground with a switch.

"Uh! Uh! Uh!" the child intoned with every blow.

Seems like the thing to do today. Yamabuki smiled to herself, remembering the farmers and their soil-breaking rites. But when Yamabuki looked closer, she realized that the child was not actually beating the earth, but instead her target was the remains of a long-dead rat too rotted for even scavengers to notice.

Leading her colt forward, Yamabuki paused only a few steps away from the child. At this, the girl looked up again. Her eyes twinkled. Unlike so many people too afraid to make eye contact with Yamabuki, the child was simply too innocent to be afraid.

Another set of live eyes.

The girl grinned.

Mochizuki snorted and pawed at the ground.

Yamabuki nodded slightly, whereupon the child, still holding the switch, brought her tiny hands and fingers to her mouth and giggled, even as Yamabuki walked right up to her and squatted down, eye to eye.

Yamabuki smiled gently in return and asked softly, "Do you have a name, girl?"

For a moment it seemed the girl was not going to answer, but then she giggled again and paused as if thinking. "Kouma!" she exclaimed at last, wrinkling her nose.

"Kouma?" Yamabuki repeated, her brows slightly raised, and laughed. "Kouma also happens to be *my* name." Yamabuki beamed, at which the child let out a cheerful laugh and offered a toothy smile.

Tiny teeth.

Just then a woman scuttled from one of the armory buildings, bowing several times as she rushed forward. The woman's kimono was made of the same material and shared the same pattern as Kouma's. Briefly Yamabuki's eyes met the other woman's, whose expression was one of embarrassment, not fear.

"She shouldn't be here at this time of day," said the woman. "I'm not sure how she got out!"

Yamabuki stood up. Little Kouma stepped back.

The older woman bowed yet again as she took the girl's hand. "Please excuse us. My husband"—she now grew flustered, sputtering—"he'll be here shortly."

At first Kouma's face filled with surprise. Then her little mouth quivered. She bit her lower lip that had begun to tremble. She waved with her free hand in protest. "Nooo!" she wailed in a high-pitched voice as the woman started to drag her away. "Horsey!" Kouma continued moaning as the woman pulled the frustrated child toward the furthest building—the one against the far cliff wall. Once inside, the sliding wooden outer door slammed shut behind them with a thud.

"It would seem someone else values you almost as much as I do . . . horsey," Yamabuki whispered with a warm grin, stroking her colt's mane.

The sound of a scraping wooden gate, opening, replaced the child's dying screech.

Twenty-Two

MEN'S ARMOR

A STOCKY BUT MUSCULAR MAN, dressed in the off-white craftsman's tunic and tall black pod-shaped hat of a smith, approached Yamabuki from the door of the largest of the buildings—the one with the highest roof, from which smoke curled through a vent hole. The man had a pleasant expression fixed on his face.

He paused about eight paces away from her and bowed formally. "Welcome, Taka-sama," he said, invoking the lofty appellation *sama* reserved for the lordly.

"You are the Katchū-shi?" she asked.

"Indeed I am. I'm Kōno Taro."

"Kōno Taro, eh?"

Taro: *eldest son*. Probably the father was the Katchū-shi before Taro was of age and then the son took over the armory. Taro could also mean *thick*. Certainly his arms were muscular. No doubt well developed.

Taro smiled earnestly, taking four steps closer, looking at her armor first. After all, what else would immediately draw an armorer's attention? Especially damaged armor. "I see you've been in a duel. May I?" He lifted his empty hands up as though he were a priest about to bestow a blessing.

She nodded and he took three more steps forward, looking even more closely at the corselet.

His eyes narrowed. "Hm. Straight and shallow cut. From a *naginata?*"

"Nodachi."

"Ha!" Taro's brows shot up. "Well," he sniffed with a look of contained admiration, "it would seem you survived."

"My opponents were not as fortunate."

"Ha-ha," he laughed perfunctorily. "All my customers seem to say the same. I've never had one of the dead come to have their armor repaired." Taro laughed at his own joke.

Yamabuki grimaced. "He did leave me this little *miyage*," she continued, running her finger along the rent in her dō.

"So you want this souvenir removed and the armor mended?"

"I am sure that is not a surprising request given your line of work."

He returned another polite smile and nodded, but his eyes remained fixed on her corselet. "Ah, Taka-sama, your armor is impressive. Not just lacquered platelets, but with metal rings sewn in. Rare."

"You fix more than leather armor, then?"

"Every type."

"How is it you boast such vast experience, yet you live in a town without a castle? Which daimyō is your patron?"

Taro shifted uneasily.

"It is complicated."

He looked fixedly at her face and then, like a mirror, he moved his finger along his own face to trace the gash that he saw on her left cheek. "Nicked by the blade?" he asked simply.

"Rock," she answered. "A gift from a dying assassin."

Taro muttered, "It's not as clean as a nick from a blade." Standing his ground, he bent forward as if to bow, but actually he looked closer. "But it's also not deep, so that's better," he said. "Hm. That'll heal without a scar, I think. You're young. You don't need my needle."

"Need your needle?"

"Not all my sewing benefits armor. Sometimes it is the wearer who is in more need of my services than what the warrior wears," he said with twinkling eyes. "Though sometimes"—he darkened as if taking in a memory—"it requires the special touch from the hot pike."

"Hot pike," Yamabuki repeated flatly.

"Hai. Seals the wound. Works better than *moe kusa*. Burning flaming herb on the skin can leave a burn-scar worse than the original cut." Kōno smiled to himself and nodded. "The pike is best when it's needed—but as I said, I doubt you'll need it."

"Let's hope it doesn't come to that," she said.

Taro chuckled darkly in agreement. "Come inside."

Yamabuki nodded. "My mount?"

Taro yelled so loud that his voice echoed off the cliff walls, "Yo-ichi!" Immediately a young man of about fourteen springs ran out of the armory.

Yamabuki pulled her naginata from the stirrup boot holder and grabbed her saddlebag. She usually would have carried it over her shoulder, but this time, owing to the rip in the bodice, she let the bag hang over her arm. She stepped away from her colt.

Yo-ichi took Mochizuki's bridle gently but firmly. "I'll take him to the stables," he said, leading the mount toward some structures at the far cliff wall.

"Yo-ichi seems well acquainted with war horses."

"It's the only kind we usually see," Kōno replied softly. "Come."

Twenty-Three

I Have Not Ever Seen
Armor Quite Like This

With its doors and windows wide open, the late-afternoon light flooded the workshop. Within, the only other people in evidence besides Yamabuki and Kōno were two youths. Their backs to her, they cried out in unison, "*Irrashai!*"—a rather informal form of welcome, which amounted to *come in.*

A gentle breeze blew through the armory, carrying the workshop's scents: the sweetness of lacquer, dye, and fresh-cut bamboo mingled with the more-acrid odor of tanning emollient, rusting iron, and burning charcoal. The planked rough pine flooring, which provided the most predominant smell, covered nearly the entire interior floor space, except for a stone-built forge near the back of the shop for working metal.

Most interesting to Yamabuki were the array of about ten wooden cage-like frames that held a variety of armor in various stages of completion, each armor piece suspended by strings and knots Open boxes of kozane, small platelets that looked like rectangular perforated coins, lay here and there. Half-stitched-together rows of kozane lay stacked in other bins, the individual plates bound by shared silk threads of vivid colors. Toward the back of the shop, away from the forge, shattered and broken armor of a wide variety of types and colors were more or less heaped into piles. The only difference in the piles was which part of the body a piece was intended. Chest protectors here. Shoulder guards there. Shin guards in yet another pile.

The two workers remained at their stations and so absorbed in their work that they had not even once bothered to look up at their visitor.

"Eiji! Fuyuki!" Taro barked. Like soldiers, the two workers leapt up and dashed forward. Yamabuki instinctively stiffened at the on-rushing men, but relaxed a bit when they paused about five paces away and bowed low before her.

She stood before them, her naginata's heel against the floor—its sharp blade gleaming in the afternoon sun. Her long sword at her right hip, hanging from cords tachi style, and her medium-length personal sword tucked through her cobalt-blue silk waist sash. She held her saddlebags with her right hand.

Taro glared at them. "Taka," he hissed low, turning his head away from them and toward Yamabuki, stretching out the word into two distinct syllables—almost in a whisper.

They again bowed as they gave a more formal greeting than earlier: "*Irrashimase*, samurai-sama!"

Taro, still severe, jabbed his finger toward the two and they bowed yet again, this time even lower. "May we assist you, Taka-sama?" they asked almost in unison.

"Help the bushi out of her armor," Taro said, softly but firmly.

The two young men took her naginata and placed it into a holder, took the long sword, still in its scabbard, and set it on a sword stand. Unlike the previous evening at the Wakatake Inn, where the two lovely young female attendants had helped Yamabuki remove all the other armor pieces before removing her helmet, Eiji and Fuyuki relieved her of her kabuto straightaway.

Nagato customs certainly are different.

And unlike the night before, Eiji and Fuyuki withheld any gasps of surprise as Yamabuki's long tresses fell to her shoulders.

Carefully the two young men undid the dō's fastenings. Together they lifted away her torn corselet and smartly brought it forward, tying it onto one of the lattice work stands. As for her undamaged armor, they meticulously—almost reverently—removed and stacked the remaining pieces.

She found herself standing in her dark-green-and-beige kimono and hakama, her personal sword never leaving her side.

Taro moved toward the broken corselet that was now strung and suspended within one of the wooden frames, which he circled in order to see the damaged chest protector from all sides before he touched it. When he finally did, he murmured, "I have not ever seen armor quite like this." He put his hand inside the corselet, running his finger over the interior metal sections.

"So, you are saying that because you haven't encountered Kadai-iwa's armor, you can't repair it?"

"Oh no. I can. It's just that I've never seen a corselet with sewn-in metal rings as backing to kozane strips. And this . . . is silk," he said, brushing his hand along the inside of the armor, "between the metal and the wearer."

She nodded.

"The rings are intact, though the stitching is ripped." He hummed to himself. "But that's just a matter of re-stitching." He looked up gleefully. "Yes. I can do it. In fact, it'll be fascinating." He looked directly at her, falling silent.

Now for the matter of payment, I suppose. She waited as she had been taught by her teachers at the Taka compound. Let the merchant speak first.

Taro said nothing.

She renewed her look of impassiveness.

He looked back.

She raised her eyebrows and tilted her head indicating that she was not going to speak.

At last he sighed and said, head bowed, but eyes up—meeting hers, "Fifty pieces of silver."

"Fifty?" she repeated flatly and tilted her head slightly.

He reddened. "I will deliver it completed in two days."

"Two days?" She let her disappointment show.

"Two days . . . two days to do it properly."

"That long? Are you working on other armor first?" She turned her head slightly, nodding toward the piles in the back of armory. "Is there a lot of work ahead of mine?"

Taro shifted uncomfortably as he looked in the direction that she indicated. With a small, embarrassed smile through clenched teeth, he answered, "Oh-ha. You come first. Those pieces?" He inclined his head toward the armor piles. "Those are payment from those who did not have coins to cover the fee."

Indeed, the armor in the back was not stored with a great deal of dignity. Now that her eyes grew even more accustomed to the dimness at the back of the shop, she noticed that many of the broken pieces were bloodstained. She let her face twist into a look of distaste.

Looted from the losers? Of course.

Yamabuki's thoughts now went back to where she left the fencing master lying resplendent, though dead, in full armor. Probably his yoroi would have fetched a handsome sum. Still, she could not imagine herself hauling around the fencing master's armor to just get some money, let alone stripping his body like she was some scavenger.

If I die in battle, will I be stripped? The thought had never really occurred to her. *I suppose I won't care because I'll be dead and my severed head in some kill-box, ready to be presented to some miscreant.*

Yamabuki's attention returned to the cage-like frames where she noticed a magnificent piece of armor on a nearby work rack. Its kozane were the deep blue of the ocean under starlight. The silk cords were emerald and white. It carried the clan crest: gentian flowers over bamboo leaves.

"And that?" she asked, indicating what could only have been an active endeavor. "Is that one ahead of mine?"

"That," he said cheerfully, "is completed. The owner's been in town for some time now. I think he's waiting for someone."

"The wounded armor seems healed," she agreed.

"It certainly wasn't when he arrived. He's young. Strong." He paused. "Handsome," he whispered. "Like your encounter with the nodachi man, his opponents did not fare well."

Handsome, eh? As for being handsome, Yamabuki's mother had often said, "A handsome man is someone who looks better than a demon."

Yamabuki sighed, "If your workmanship is as good as you claim, I will pay you what you ask."

"Ha!" Taro bowed formally. "I am honored."

She nodded. "One more question. Does the town have a swordsmith?"

Taro shook his head. "It did . . . until three summers ago."

"No work?" she asked skeptically.

"Oh, plenty of work." He whispered, "*Tōsō.*"

"The pox?"

Taro nodded slowly.

"So who sharpens swords now?"

"Alas, I've had to take that on."

"Alas?"

"My skill is in making iron things that blunt and block weapons, not so much in making steel things that are sharp."

She stepped to the weapons rack to retrieve her scabbard and withdrew the long blade halfway. Even in the shadowy shop, its edge flashed. She lifted the cutting edge horizontally for his inspection. "This is Tiger Claw. The damage is from this morning," she said simply. "What can you do with this? And be careful."

"I may not be an expert polisher, but I know my way around swords. I rarely, if ever, nick myself."

"You certainly do not want to nick yourself with this. Though I've taken great care to wipe it clean, it might still have vestiges of fugu."

"Paralyzing poison?"

"Let's say my assailants had, well . . . a bit of imagination."

"Ah." He bowed to Tiger Claw. "May I ask who made your sword?"

She bestowed a satisfied expression. "Yukiyasu."

"Ha!" he exclaimed. "This work certainly is too good for me."

She frowned.

"The last smith—the one who died—he was an apprentice to Arinari Ichi. Fifth-generation sword makers. You've no doubt you've heard of the Arinari?"

"Arinari? No."

Taro seemed surprised. He sniffed. "The Arinari are swordsmiths to the Emperor."

"If your dead swordsmith was associated with ones so illustrious, then why was he in Minezaki instead of living in wealth and ease in Heian-kyō."

Taro shifted awkwardly. "Ah, well . . . like many people in this town, matters proved—how shall I say this—difficult for him in the capital, and so he made his way south to where he could earn a living."

"Nevertheless, my blade needs to be sharpened."

Taro bowed in acquiescence. "Since I am not accomplished as a polisher, I will take this on and include it as part of the original fee."

Yamabuki bowed slightly, accepting the offer. "Your apprentices. Do they know this town well?"

"Ah! My sons? Hai."

"They would know if strangers come to town?"

Taro's mouth twisted. "We are at the intersection of two great highways. Lots of strangers pass up and down North Road. There are others who come along the East-West Passage. On most any day there are more strangers in this town than people who live here, though most of the townspeople have been out readying the fields."

"I am looking for a stranger who has but one eye. See anyone like that recently?"

Eiji and Fuyuki looked at one another and shook their heads. "Everyone has two eyes in this town," Fuyuki said at last, "even the blind ones."

"I am on the lookout for an assassin—a clever one. He goes by the name Saburo."

"Ah. The fugu. A *shinobi*?" Taro asked quietly. "An assassin's trick."

"The last time I saw him, Saburo was wearing the clothes of a fisherman, but it was probably a disguise. If you see a man with but one eye, all his teeth, and decidedly black hair, you will tell me?"

"Ah." Taro nodded.

She frowned. "Don't confront him. He's extremely dangerous. Just come and tell me and I shall take care of it."

Taro nodded and raised his wrist toward Eiji and Fuyuki, which meant they were to comply with Yamabuki's request.

She fully sheathed Tiger Claw and handed it to Taro.

Taro accepted the sheathed sword and then grew intent. "This can be a dangerous town. It's not from just a one-eyed man."

She tapped her shorter sword, Tiger Cub, which remained in its scabbard tucked through her waist sash. "Does this town have an inn? Food? Saké?"

Taro exchanged looks with his sons. They were polite glances, but she could see they revealed concern. Taro took in a quick breath. "Oh, it does. The house with the dark-green banner, but a Lady such as yourself would do better than staying at the saké house." He shifted uncomfortably with a look of embarrassment. "The saké house has rooms, but they are"—he paused as if searching for words—"not so good. The only kind of women who stay there are the kind who serve male patrons, and it isn't saké they serve, if you take my meaning."

She laughed inwardly. *I left three dead men in the road today, my armor is ripped open, my blade edge is battle worn, and he thinks I'm too delicate to be told outright that there are yahochi in this town.*

"I can make do."

"Well." Taro nodded to himself and said simply, "What if you stay here. At the Ledge. We have food, such as it is, and a warm place to sleep. Part of the fifty silver pieces."

"Stay here? In the armory?"

"There's a small guest quarters. Not used anymore. My daughter will show you. It's quiet and out of the way. Even a two-eyed man would have trouble finding it."

"Very well. I don't want to be too far from Mochizuki, anyway."

"Very wise in this town," Kōno nodded. "Mari!" he cried out. "The guest house is simple . . ." he said apologetically.

"No need to say more. So long as the bed has no *mushi*, I will be satisfied."

Taro gulped and nodded.

TWENTY-FOUR
THE HOUSE

A PRETTY WOMAN maybe two or three years younger than Yamabuki came to the shop's open back entry and stood, shyly waiting. Yamabuki flashed her a small smile of encouragement. Taro then turned and burst into a grin. "Ah!" he exclaimed, waving the girl over. "Come. Come. My daughter, Mari," he said, more or less introducing her.

Yamabuki immediately noticed that Mari was dressed in a kimono graced by a pattern which was a mixture of orange shades and then decorated with small blue and red butterflies. It was identical to the kimono worn by Kouma and her young mother.

Mari walked closer and bowed to the warrior, who returned a slight nod.

"The samurai will be staying in . . ." Taro began, but then paused as if searching for a word, "the House."

Mari blinked and stared almost blankly. Then something seemed to enter her thoughts. "Ha! Hai. Hai," she said rapidly. "The House!" she repeated. "Of course. Yes."

"She will be our honored guest for two nights." Taro's eyes brightened with pride. "Share our food with her. See she wants for nothing." Mari bowed, indicating that she understood. Yamabuki and the armorer exchanged bows, his much lower than hers.

Mari took one of the small brazier lamps from near the armory's hearth and then led Yamabuki out a side exit, giving Yamabuki her first complete view of the back. She scrutinized the surroundings and the four smaller structures tucked away behind the armory in the expansive open area.

Two naturally perpendicular vertical rock walls, almost like those of a granite castle, boxed-in the mesa. The two walls—one on the west and the other on the north—created a notch. The remaining side was open to the eastern sky and an almost-vertical drop-off. In effect, it was a cul-de-sac, Ledge Road, coming in from the south.

Like all things in life, the location's advantages were also its weakness. The natural terrain guarded three sides and thus there was only one way in or out—Ledge Road, making it both a fortress and a trap.

On the ledge itself, two buildings, likely the family living quarters, faced east-southeast, which probably meant that they caught the morning sun and could be counted on to remain in warmth and light for most of the day. They were close, but not too close, to the night-soil pits. Not too far to walk at night.

Yamabuki had become more than acquainted with the latter contrivances over her last ten days on the road—nothing like the indoor boxes of sand at the Taka compound. Out in the countryside, these primitive slots were dug in the earth and had timber rails that ran along each side. To relieve herself she would have to brace with her hands, her hind end naked in the wind, poised over someone else's *kuso*. She thought the smell at the Taka compound was bad, but these ditches were indeed ripe. But no matter, she would be able to find them at night, if only by their smell.

The third structure was built at the furthest end of the Ledge, against the far rock wall. What did it conceal? Possibly a secret set of caves? A back way out? It was where Kouma and her mother had disappeared.

Secret way or not, the stables stood next to the third building. She took some comfort in the fact her horse would remain the furthest in and somewhat hidden, though she pitied anyone else who would try to ride the temperamental colt. From where she stood, she saw Mochizuki munching on some feed while Yo-ichi brushed the horse's coat. A good boy, taking care of the colt.

The last building, the one Taro had referred to as the "House," was at the base of the towering cliff on the left, immediately be-hind the armory and the farthest from the night-soil pit.

The House had an eastern exposure, but being further from the drop-off, likely was less sunny in the morning. This guest house, therefore, was designed to allow "good people," unlike the com-moners, to sleep past dawn.

As the sun settled behind the west ridge, darkness quickly spread over the cluster of buildings. The mountain air dampened and brought an extra chill to the spring evening.

"This way," Mari said as she stepped onto what could only be called a poor man's version of an *engawa*. Unlike the outer walk-ways at the Taka compound, where as many as six people could walk abreast, this one was hardly wide enough for one person, but the propriety it added suggested that anyone who stayed in the guest house must be important.

Made of pine wood with a thatched roof, the entire footprint of the dwelling was smaller than Yamabuki's sleeping chamber in her own private estate house.

Mari put her shoulder into the heavy wooden outer door, which scraped against the rails. "It has been a while," she apologized. "I'll sweep and oil the rail right after you've settled in."

Mari kicked off her simple sandals and stepped inside. She put the lamp on a small stone pillar—a wise precaution to contain things that burned, especially when they were brought into all-wood-and-straw buildings.

Right behind, Yamabuki removed her boots and followed.

The guest house was not much more than a large room. The floor planks were smooth, but not lacquered—thus they absorbed the light—and with the building in the shadow of the cliff, the interior was almost night-like, but thanks to the brazier, cheerful enough.

"I'm sure this place is not what you are accustomed to. Not for a fine Lady such as yourself."

Yamabuki shook her head, her lips pressed together, to say that everything was well. There were no words of complaint forthcoming.

"My father. He's a good man. Not like the low-lifes who loiter around this town."

"A town of low-lifes." Yamabuki laughed softly. Every one of the towns and places she had stayed over the last ten nights was more or less filled with despicable people. She had given up the life of the Court to discover the true world, and now she most certainly had.

"You have heard the rumors?" Mari looked quizzically before her mouth drew into a thin line. "Young Hiromoto and his followers are battling with the Ōuchi."

"I've heard of him. Yes." Yamabuki nodded.

Mari hesitated. "Maybe I shouldn't be saying such things to a Taka samurai but, as you are a woman warrior traveling on her own through this district, I have to speak. Many warriors are using the rebellion as an excuse to loot. They don't fight in the battles. They come in after the defeated run away and the winners go in chase. 'Without the rule of law, the lawless rule,' at least that's what everyone's saying."

Yamabuki put Tiger Cub on a low stand near the bedding. "I will be careful." She laughed softly. "As you can see," Yamabuki said, sweeping her hand across her bloodied riding-skirt, "I have had my own encounters with low-lifes." Yamabuki straightened. "You said something about food," she said, for her stomach had begun to churn.

"Ah! Please wait." Mari bowed and disappeared.

Yamabuki sat down on the sleeping mat.

Mari was not long in returning. "Please." She set down a bowl before Yamabuki. Millet—*kibi.*

Mari poured hot wine into a cup.

Kushi! Yamabuki tried not to let her face show her disappointment with the beverage, a rustic's form of saké. *Fermented barley sap. Hardly fit to drink.* Kushi meant "mysterious thing." *The mystery is how anyone can stomach it.*

Mari stepped outside momentarily and returned with a colorful bundle. "Samurai-sama. It's still the Hour of the Monkey."

Yamabuki nodded. And so?

"I have brought you a kimono." Mari smiled. "I can wash and press your riding clothes. This kimono is fresh. And if you put it on before the Hour of the Bird, then changing to new clothes won't bring any bad luck."

"Bad luck?" Yamabuki almost made a comment about the luck of the day, but then let it go. She was alive and maybe that had been a matter of luck . . . as well as years of drilling in the fencing hall.

"The material is like yours," Yamabuki said, touching the bundle.

"Hai. Our family kimono. All the women wear the same pattern. I hope that this doesn't offend you."

Yamabuki shook her head. The idea of getting to wear clean and fresh clothing appealed to her. Though not common, the clothing was not especially regal, either. As if she could read Yamabuki's mind, Mari said, "I saw you wore royal yellow. We have nothing so fine, but this garment is warm. The nights are cold here in the high hills."

"Cold in spring?"

"Travelers are usually the first to notice. I saw your bearskin fur boots. Keep them close."

Mari dropped a glowing ember from her brazier into the *irori*, then from a box, never getting her hands dirty, she poured a few coal lumps on top. The cold coals in the fire pit began to glow.

"You know how to move fires." Yamabuki gave her a small nod as the irori warmed the room.

"It is my duty that the flames do not ever go out," said Mari as she helped Yamabuki into the Kōno clan kimono. She took Yamabuki's clothing, vowing to have them completely cleaned by morning. Mari ended by asking if there was anything else Yamabuki needed, pledging to be of service. The warrior said all she wanted to do was rest for the night.

By herself, Yamabuki took stock. The room was so small, it was not fit for much more than sleeping.

How can one sleep after this?

Indeed, it had been a horrible day.

"It's time," she mumbled to herself. She reached into her saddlebag.

Twenty-Five

The Pillow Book of a Samurai

RIGHT NEAR THE TOP of the saddlebags, her fingers found the green-gray ink stone. Though made of granite, it was quite thin and therefore not overly heavy, yet its surface proved hard enough to crush and grind even the sturdiest of ink sticks. The stone's edges were framed in thin-lacquered bamboo the same green as her armor. She poured a small measure of water onto the tray, after which she began to grind the *sumi* against the smooth surface. The tiny pieces of ink dissolved, turning the water black.

She opened a tightly sealed wooden box that bore the Taka mon. The box was filled with parchment that had been cut into almost perfect rectangles.

She removed the top sheet of rice paper and placed it in front of her, then looked over at the half-finished bowl of kibi, and the barely touched cup of kushi, before finally lifting her dry brush. The blank parchment looked yellow by lamplight. She dipped her brush into the stone tray and swirled its bristles. She suspected that today she would need as many as ten sheets. She stared into the parchment's emptiness.

Where to begin?

She would start with the date. Even without Nakagawa's incessant admonitions about this, she knew that unless she recorded things right after they happened, she would begin to forget the precise flow of events.

By her celestial calculations, today was the fifteenth day of New Life Month, the Day of the Tiger, a day said to be one of coldness and cruelty. It certainly had been that. *Special numbers. Lucky days. Well-aspected directions. What rubbish!* It was as Nakagawa said, "We make our own luck."

Unable to gather herself to write, perhaps she would start with something trivial. She began to sketch a bird. A taka. It started off well enough until it came to the beak and ended up looking more like a pelican. She crumpled the paper in her fist. She tossed it into the fire pit. The coals turned the edges dark. They curled as they smoldered, red, then burst into yellow flame.

Maybe she needed to translate a poem before starting something as formidable as setting this particular day's events down in her pillow book.

Yamabuki understood the writing of people of the Sòng Dynasty—the people who lived across the Leeward Sea, in the delta, tributaries, and lands along the Yellow River—the Yangzi. She was always calmed when she converted their ancient pictograms into her own native tongue. It was a puzzle as much as anything. The written language of Akitsushima strung letters together to form words. The pictograms of the Sòng Dynasty assembled ideas. This subtle difference was the challenge to the translator, and solving such puzzles centered her as much as any meditation could.

She opened her collection of pictogram poems that Nakagawa

had given her. Many of them predated the Sòng Dynasty, going back to a time those lands were known as Qin.

She found an ancient poem by an anonymous writer, meaning it likely was written by a woman, for men's names were always remembered, while women's were always hard to recall. But Yamabuki didn't care. Whoever wrote it captured the mood of the day.

She set down a few lines, as always adjusting the setting to suit her purposes.

Tall cliffs look down on the narrow lane of greening trees
The sun slips behind the mountain as a cold breeze floats across the hill
A small girl stands in the road
Boys run through the village and urge one another on
I hear them calling, but I do not understand their words

She paused. Hearing a word was not enough. To truly understand a word, one had to see how it was written, and once written, a word might take on an entirely different meaning than was at first suspected.

She thought of her handmaid. Before Yamabuki saw her thirteenth spring, she was permitted to take one personal handmaid into her service. Exactly who, was to be her choice. And to almost everyone's amazement, Yamabuki chose a younger girl named Tomoko.

The word "tomoko" is often written using calligraphy for the word "companion." After all, it is written as two side-by-side moons:

朋

So, at first, everyone took the name to mean "handmaid," an ap-

propriate name for a servant girl, even if Tomoko was of the aristocratic kuge, the class of the highest position.

There is another calligraphy that is also pronounced "tomoko":

And this was the way young Tomoko had been taught to sign
her name from the time she could first hold a brush. Yamabuki
believed this calligraphy to be accurate. Her signature was a combination of three other characters:

arrow 矢

mouth 口

and sun 日

. . . thus together they meant: The "knowing sun," or "she who
speaks directly every day." The "one who speaks with brilliant di-
rectness." In short, the calligraphy for "wisdom."

The two girls, princess and handmaid, were not symbolized by
two pale masculine moons. They were girls of the sun, and the sun
was a Goddess, perhaps the greatest of them, and despite their
supposed differences within the strict ranks of the kuge hierarchy,
the two girls immediately bonded, for Tomoko shared the same
flashing eyes, infectious smile, and quick mind as Yamabuki.

Some years later, when she learned that the Court elders at the
time had strongly opposed Tomoko, Yamabuki was aghast and
appalled. What did the Council care who would attended to her
personal needs? What business of theirs was it who would help
dress and undress her? But care they did.

Yamabuki was also later told that the Council had gone to the
daimyō to suggest Yamabuki's selection was rash and unschooled
and should be rescinded. They urged Tomoko be replaced as
quickly as possible. They went so far as to say Yamabuki should

be assigned an older handmaid. Someone not *too* old, but nevertheless more mature than Tomoko and much wiser in the wiles
of womanhood. Someone like Lady Taka's youngest and newest
handmaid, Rei, who, though marked by the pox, had the time, tal-
ent, and charm to guide Yamabuki in laying out the enticements
needed to win a husband of promise and importance. And if she
were lucky, Yamabuki might even gain the attentions of a man
from a neighboring clan whose babies she would bear. Sons! An
alliance through marriage which would produce the future ruler
of not just Ō-Utsumi Prefecture but a combination of three or
maybe even four of the provinces of the southern-most isle.

Lord Taka listened, nodded thoughtfully, and told the Council
that he appreciated what they had to say, and then let Yamabuki's
choice stand. How could the warlord countermand his soon-to-be
adult daughter's first decision?

Looking back, Yamabuki now appreciated how things were far
more complicated than she ever knew.

TWENTY-SIX

THE TWENTY-SIXTH DAY OF CLOTHES-LAYER MONTH

FIVE YEARS EARLIER, on the first day of the Second Year of Nin-an, the daimyō, Lord Taka, warlord and undisputed ruler of Ō-Utsumi Prefecture, received a prophecy: His personal astrologer said that the heavens would align on the second-to-last day of Clothes-Layer Month, making it an especially favorable day for the warlord's twelve-year-old daughter and sole surviving child. On that day in that month, when the waning moon would shrink to but a shard, it would be the vernal equinox of the lunar year.

The auspiciousness of the first day of the time known as Shunbun came as no surprise, for the daimyō already had been told that the day would be lucky for his daughter. Earlier he had consulted with Minister-in-Chief Nakagawa, her tutor, and Nakagawa's calculations had already confirmed that *that* day would be celestially well aspected. But more importantly, by Lord Taka's personal calculations, the day could be politically useful.

When the daimyō, who sometimes also went by the title General Moroto, asked for a report on the progress of his daughter's studies, Lord Nakagawa said that she was making significant strides. She was quickly learning the spoken and written language of the Sòng Dynasty. "Yamabuki is becoming a promising translator," Nakagawa offered. "Her calligraphy is exceptional for a child of twelve."

"Fourteen," Moroto said softly, "come the vernal equinox."

Nakagawa raised a brow. Everyone of importance knew that Yamabuki had gasped her first breath of life inside the Itō Palace in the capital during the Second Year of Kyū-ju, coming into the world just three days before the Dark Moon of the eleventh month, when the nights were the longest and darkest. Strictly speaking, as of the vernal equinox, it would barely be twelve years and four months since her birth. Yet, according to the ancient convention, all girls' ages were perfunctorily increased on the vernal equinox, not on the anniversary of their birth. By counting in this way, Moroto could say that Yamabuki would be thirteen come spring. And by adding the nominal one year that all children were automatically granted at birth for their time in the womb, her age could be stretched to fourteen.

Moroto interrupted Nakagawa's cogitation. "How are Yamabuki's sword studies progressing?"

"She's an instinctive fighter," Nakagawa answered. "Fast reflexes. Focused. Aware of her surroundings. She moves in an almost free-form dance while fighting."

The daimyō nodded. "I've noticed. That can't be taught. Comes from inside her. She training with sharp steel?"

"Almost always. She handles a medium sword almost as well as most adults do."

"She ready for long sword?"

Nakagawa nodded. "I doubt she'll hurt herself, or anyone else for that matter. She keeps control. And she's strong. Though at times she's a bit unpredictable."

Instead of a disapproving look, the daimyō merely smiled. "Good."

Twenty-Seven

An Arranged Marriage

I N THE PRIVACY OF their bedchamber, the daimyō shared his innermost thoughts with his only wife, Yamabuki's birth mother, Lady Taka. In the truest sense, she was his most trusted, loyal, and honest advisor. Throughout their twenty years of marriage, they had always spoken frankly to one another. And now she would be the first to hear of his plans for their daughter.

He began, "I've been thinking about the succession of the Taka lineage."

Lady Taka smiled politely.

Moroto paced around the chamber as though he was rallying his troops. "The counselors have again been reminding me that we've no male heir and no male successor." His mouth drawn, he said, "The Council is pressing me to take a second wife."

For a moment, Lady Taka looked shocked. "That *never* works!" She sounded stunned. "It becomes a contest of lineages and will rip the clan apart. It'll unknot the alliance between the Taka and the Itō. You yourself have said why it would not work even in the best of circumstances." Lady Taka's voice grew stronger, with an edge of annoyance that she rarely let herself reveal in front of the daimyō, even in private. "I've given you *male* children. It was the Gods who took them."

"I do not wish an additional wife," the daimyō said firmly. "And even if I were to take such a one, and if she were fertile, and if the child was male, and if the child was perfect born, and if the child survived, it would be years before such a child could rule in his own right."

"I don't suppose you pointed that out to the Council."

The daimyō frowned. "They've argued that a regent could rule. But I've no use for such fictions—a mere pretense that a *kugutsu* rules when actually someone else moves the puppet's arms, eyes, and mouth. On the other hand, some have suggested that if something happened to me, you could step into the role of warlord."

"A dowager warlord, like up in the north of Honshu?" Lady Taka folded her hands. "That sounds to me like Nakagawa talking. I think he's the only one who would think that way."

"Empress Jingū led an army across the Great Sea—and she personally led troops in battle while carrying Hachiman, the War God, in her womb."

"That was a millennium ago. Jingū was half my age when she went into battle. I hope you'll outlive me, husband, but if not, I only hope I do not live long afterward. Besides, I only have Itō blood and you know that *that* would be immediately denounced. Whoever rules after you must be someone with Taka blood."

The daimyō smiled sadly and sweetly. "I married you because I knew you would not be an ornament."

Lady Taka hummed softly. "Well." She looked at him directly with an equally small smile, but one that was coy. "It was . . . an *arranged* marriage, was it not?"

"Before we met, I already knew you were an accomplished warrior in your own right. The Itō sent me a drawing of your likeness."

Lady Taka nodded slowly as if remembering.

"And when I saw you," he said, "I instantly realized that the drawing didn't do you the slightest justice. Our daughter carries your beauty. It's why she's sure to find a husband. But," he said, "I have to say *something* to the Council, even if I refuse. Otherwise, the Council will simmer and maybe even plan in secret about what to do when I am no more."

"You suspect they plan a coup?"

"No." The daimyō pulled in a deep breath. "At least not at the moment. However, Atsumichi's name's been brought up."

"The boy's a fool!"

"Fool or not, he's my brother's son."

"If Atsumichi were to become the next in line, it would make Tachibana the father of the next daimyō. My stomach turns at the thought."

"Some say it's the logical choice. Some believe, the only choice."

"We could try again." Lady Taka looked into her husband's eyes. "Maybe we could have another boy. This time the Gods may help him survive."

The daimyō stopped pacing. "We can't wait, hoping for luck. We must act now. I have a strategy."

Lady Taka brightened.

"I want to raise Yamabuki to majority at the vernal equinox." The daimyō's words were more of a pronouncement than the expression of a wish.

"In two months? She's barely twelve."

"Boys can be elevated to adulthood at twelve."

"But girls have to wait until they are at least fourteen before they're recognized as grown. Mature enough to be able to have children—" She nodded, finishing her sentence without saying the obvious.

"That is not our purpose here, is it?" General Moroto offered. "Atsumichi's slightly younger than Yamabuki, yes?"

Lady Taka nodded. "Yes, though not by much. He was born in the late summer after Yamabuki."

"Nine months, to be exact. And yet, this coming year, Atsumichi will be twelve and by any reckoning can rightfully be raised to adulthood. What we have to do is establish our own daughter as an adult before that happens."

"How?"

"At the equinox she will have seen her thirteenth spring. And adding the pre-birth year makes her fourteen. You just said girls can be raised to majority at fourteen."

Lady Taka pursed her lips. "Boys can come of age at twelve years old because they can shoulder a spear," she said. "But a girl? It's all about having the rhythm with the moon."

"A girl can begin her flow as early as twelve," the daimyō whispered.

Lady Taka stopped to look carefully at her husband. "Is there something you know that I do not? Has she begun to—" Lady Taka broke off, her hand slowly moving to her mouth.

The daimyō set his jaw, a sign everyone knew meant the warlord wanted something and that he would not be turned aside, irrespective of any facts. "In the absence of a male heir, a female heir could succeed me . . . us."

Lady Taka looked worried. "Mark my words, if you make our

daughter the heir, once we're gone someone will put a knife into her the moment she turns her back. Maybe sooner."

"Then we must make sure she learns how not to leave her back exposed. Besides, if someone thinks she's in the way of their aims, they'll kill her, no matter. She'll stand a better chance in her battle gear than in kimono."

"No woman, no matter how much battle gear she wears, will be perceived as a ruler. They'll sneer. They'll say she wears the armor for show. A costume. A charade. Nothing more." Lady Taka continued darkly, "The household guard might follow her in defending the castle while the army is away. Or she might lead a detachment in a larger battle commanded by her husband. But men rarely, and never readily, follow women. That does not come to a woman simply by putting on yoroi."

"You do not need to tell me that," said Lord Taka, irritation in his voice. "It goes the same for men. You think my troops follow me because I put on armor?"

The daimyō drew in a breath to calm himself. He was not cross with his wife. Indeed, she was not saying anything he had not already considered. It was that she gave voice to the words he had not even dared whisper to himself.

He continued, "If we let Yamabuki grow, become independent, then, as a ruler in her own right, we'll find her a husband. A good match, not some adventurer who'll throw her aside the moment he's finished adding the Taka lands by bedding her."

Lady Taka looked deeply into the daimyō's eyes. "Will she listen?" She pondered, taking a long breath. "If we start grooming her to be more than a bride, we may well get more than we bargained for. You may well get a female warlord out of it. She's already headstrong.

Too headstrong. She may well decide to go her own way. Though you may get what you ask for, you may not get what you think."

"Girls *always* do the right thing. They *always* listen to their parents," said General Moroto with a smile of reassurance.

Lady Taka's eyebrows shot up, unreassured. "They do, do they?"

"In the end, yes."

"You're *so* certain of our daughter."

"It's now *you* who sounds quite certain."

"I ought to. I was once just like her. Young. I didn't know anything." Lady Taka let out a deep sigh and shook her head slowly and thoughtfully. "Well. I suppose she'll be better off training than preening. You're my husband and I'll do as asked."

Moroto brightened. He had his way as always, and yet he could not help but see the apprehension in her eyes.

The daimyō assembled the Council, bringing the high-ranking warriors and the important Court nobles together. In a commanding voice, he informed them that their attendance would be required for a momentous ceremony to be held on the first day of the fourth solar stem. In the Great Audience Hall, before all those assembled, the warlord's last surviving child would be lifted to majority. She would undertake *mogi*, one of the most colorful rites of passage.

Not long after, Yamabuki was told that, by tradition, at mogi a Taka Princess sings the epic poem, *The Tale of the Taka*. At once, Tomoko pledged to help Yamabuki memorize the poem that took almost a half hour to recite in full.

Though coming of age was supposed to be a day of great import and joy, in reality Yamabuki felt anxious about going through a rite reserved for girls who were considerably older than she.

It seemed that everyone had an opinion about the sudden on-rush of events. These musings were mostly repeated in private. Having a cheerful handmaid who knew when to listen and when to speak, who could funnel information, gave Yamabuki insight that she otherwise might never have had.

Tomoko repeated all the whispers. "Your uncle is not saying much, but his wives have a lot to say, and little of it good, especially Yoma, who calls you the 'girl whose breasts have not budded,' and that you are too young to have mogi because you can't have babies yet."

Yamabuki let out a huge sigh and looked heavenward. "She's Tachibana's first wife and never has anything kind to say about anyone except Atsumichi." Yamabuki frowned. "If my uncle had been first-born, instead of my father, wouldn't Yoma be happy now!"

"Of course, because then *she'd* be the great Lady Taka instead of it being your mother."

The girls laughed and tried to forget the churlish whispers as best they could. The mogi was going to happen, regardless. The daimyō had spoken.

TWENTY-EIGHT

THE DOLL IS DRESSED

T HE VERNAL EQUINOX dawned. Yamabuki and Tomoko were told to wait in the Great Chamber of Plum Blossoms for the ceremonial preparations. They looked at one another, at first saying little. For the most part, the two girls pretended to study the fine, ornate white and pink blooms painted on the room's walls and screens.

Built to withstand the elements along the strategic windward bluffs, the Taka compound was influenced by—some said adapted from—the disparate T'ang and Toi styles of architecture.

The architecture found elsewhere in semi-tropical parts of Akitsushima had rooms that were separated merely by *kichō* drapes or *misu* screens. Flimsy fabric that allowed conversations to flow over their tops. Almost anyone could eavesdrop.

On the other hand, the Taka compounds halls were partitioned into various chambers that could be closed off by sliding panels that reached to the ceiling. These rooms were enclaves unto themselves. The heavy wooden walls on rails also kept the interior warm and private.

Alone, with the doors closed to the Great Chamber of Plum

Blossoms, the two girls were certain that they could not be overheard.

Yamabuki asked at last, "What are the whispers about today?"

"Some of the women, and not just the younger ones, have been gossiping that today you're being elevated to the status of a *boy*."

"A boy?"

"Yes. Since you're having your mogi in your twelfth year, they're saying your father plans to make you the next daimyō."

"Everyone knows that I'm a girl," Yamabuki protested. "My father's not going to make me a warlord. Is he?" Yamabuki, perhaps for the first time, was seeing something for herself that was plain to almost everyone else. "No one's said—"

Tomoko whispered, "Everyone also knows that there have been women emperors, and not just Jingū. Kōken was an Empress."

"Four hundred years ago." An ancient idea, Yamabuki argued.

Tomoko laughed playfully. "You do know your history of the lineages, so I'm sure you also know that even today women daimyō rule entire prefectures." She dropped her voice even lower, holding her mouth as though she wanted no one to be able to read her lips. "In the north."

Yamabuki frowned. "There's only one in the entire Empire, and she's a rustic. A dowager. And everyone says she's homely with warts all over her face, and has hair as short as a nun's."

"Maybe so. But she's a warlord in her own right, and they say she's fighting the barbarians, and they say she commands just like her husband did, and that she personally leads her troops into battle, and that she's *winning*," said Tomoko, all in one breath.

Yamabuki paused, as if thinking on what Tomoko had just said, and then asked, "Is there anything more they're saying?"

"People are saying that you have no brothers."

"So?"

"Well, *that* more than anything else means you'll be made the next warlord. It can't be someone from your mother's clan."

"Some of the courtiers hate the Itō clan, don't they?"

"Not everyone." Tomoko beamed, for her own kuge lineage, too, was partly Itō.

A sharp sound broke through the room. The main door opened so quickly it almost flew off the rails. The corridor leading into the chamber was crowded with dark figures standing back in shadows.

"Lady Taka!" a female voice cried out.

Yamabuki's mother stepped forward into the full light. Wearing multilayer kimono and courtly make-up, she could not have looked more perfect had she been presented to the Emperor Himself. Yamabuki immediately met her mother's gaze. Their quick glance reflected everything that was special between mother and daughter. A secret not to be shared outside of themselves.

Yamabuki and Tomoko fell to their knees, their foreheads to the floor, kowtowing before the lofty personage, mother or not.

"Denka!" they uttered in unison.

As though she were in command on a battlefield, Lady Taka carried a silver *tessen* of seventeen iron folds that symbolized her authority. She was followed by eight *nyōbō*, her personal handmaids who, like Lady Taka, wore rice-white make-up and had blackened their teeth. Their carefully brushed hair was so long that it reached the floor. The sounds of silk kimono, hems rubbing, hissed like the music of silk strings as the handmaids carried in armloads of the finest fabrics. Behind them, at least another twenty women of the household staff, in almost martial formation, scurried up with even more bundles of material of the most exquisite colors and patterns.

The scuffle of so many feet over wooden floors was the only other sound. Normally among such a throng there would have been the murmur of many voices, but today there was only one.

"Enough bowing!" Lady Taka lifted her hand. "Stand up. Bowing will have to wait—there will be plenty of time for bowing before this day is over. Much to do. Too little time to do it."

The temple bell began to toll. Four strikes reverberated through the compound. The Hour of the Snake: the part of the day when the rising red and orange of the sun vanished; a time when the orb was above the trees, but far below mid-heaven. Today the four familiar bell peals carried a sense of urgency. Yamabuki shook her head, trying to cast away any feelings of dread. She knew that she had to be dressed and ready by the Hour of the Sheep—when the sun had left mid-heavens to start its western descent.

Though Lady Taka seemed composed, Yamabuki could sense her mood, something her mother had never successfully been able to conceal from her daughter, even before the child could walk.

This was to be Yamabuki's great day, yet the older handmaids paid surprisingly little attention to her, the invitee of honor. The nyōbō, bigger than either of the two girls, moved toward Yamabuki, gently nudging Tomoko aside.

Yamabuki shot a quick look to her mother. *Why are they so rude?* But her mother was looking away, busily instructing some of the confused and overwhelmed porters who had never carried so many things at once. Without wasting a moment, two nyōbō proceeded to pull off Yamabuki's tunic and then her white, rich silk under-sheath, leaving Yamabuki naked and shivering. She tried to cover herself with her hands and arms. True, the household staff were expected to dress and undress those whom they served, and to help them in the privy, but never should Yamabuki have been exposed in front of other people. Only Tomoko was permitted to glimpse Yamabuki totally undressed, let alone touch and disrobe her. The nyōbō acted indifferently, as if they had every right, yet Yamabuki felt she was on show. Only because her mother was present and in charge did Yamabuki stay quiet.

The nyōbō exchanged secretive glances, observing the correctness of the gossip: Yamabuki's body was not yet fully a womanly form—still a slip of a girl, a mere child.

Tomoko seethed. Her expression turned black. She blanched and then flushed. Without being invited, she turned on her heel and ran up to one of the entourage.

"A *shitagi!*" she demanded.

One of the porters vapidly raised a rich red silk version of the under-kimono. Tomoko paused over the color—was it even a shitagi?—then, deciding it was, tore it out of the porter's hands and dashed back to Yamabuki. Instantly, Tomoko helped Yamabuki into it.

"An adult woman of nobility wears a shitagi of *red* silk," Rei said dryly, adding, "Red silk. Helps you with your *monthly* pain." The older handmaid then cast a small, sour smile toward the younger one. Tomoko turned her nose up, too angry to look back and too polite to say anything.

"Shhh," Yamabuki whispered to Tomoko. "Don't listen." Yamabuki curled her lip. "Rei's shitagi is probably brown like moldering leaves. Wormwood." Both girls giggled.

"I see we are ready," Lady Taka announced to everyone, though

she glared at her daughter, whose sharp words must have carried
to a mother whose ears were quite attuned to the child's voice.
"Let us begin!" She flicked the fan, which made a smart snapping
sound of metal-on-metal.

With Yamabuki's under-kimono in place, the trying on of kimono layers began in earnest. Like a doll, Yamabuki was dressed,
undressed, and re-dressed while Lady Taka pronounced which, if
any, of her weavers' and tailors' creations were worthy of her daughter. Lady Taka decided quickly: This kimono. No! That kimono.
Now another one. No! None of them. Now yet another one.

Yamabuki was still in the midst of trying on kimono when nine
bell strikes sounded. The first quarter of the Hour of the Horse,
the noon span, had started. Though at first Yamabuki had donned
the exquisite garments with some relish, after a while she began to
grow weary of the continuous changes of costume, especially since
more than once she was forced to give up some of the patterns and
colors she found most fetching. Not only kimono, but Yamabuki
was also fitted with shoulder pads and stiff-starched draping trains
so hardened with vegetable extracts that they seemed more wood
than cloth. The heavy ends of the kimono sleeves were rolled back
and the interior dabbed with a thick rice mash to glue the cuffs
out of the way.

"Let it dry. Don't move," said a nyōbō.

Finally, with the sun moving into position directly overhead,
Yamabuki stood wrapped like an overstuffed puppet in the
karaginumo, "the T'ang-style sheath and skirt." She felt as if the
layers weighed almost as much as she.

"One layer for each of your years," said one of the handmaids.

In actuality, all told, there were more than twelve layers.

"Now. Move," Lady Taka whispered loudly. "You have to move." She nodded encouragingly.

Yamabuki took a halting half step. "I can't move in this. It binds."

"You well know it's meant to be that way. A woman of station doesn't stride like she's galloping back to the stable. She takes small, stately steps, or she won't be taken for the lady that she is."

"It's so heavy."

Lady Taka ignored the protest and, with a sweep of the hand, summoned one of the porters, who came forward with a flawlessly polished and smooth steel mirror.

Yamabuki gazed at herself. She was indeed enticing. The kimono colors included white blossom, cherry blossom, straw, fern, leaves, burnt orange, plum, sunflower, and rust: the colors found in nature during all the seasons. Likely it would have been easier to say which colors were not included—black, red, blue, yellow: "official" colors associated with governmental rank.

The patterns of Yamabuki's kimono were varied, yet fit together as a whole. Everyone, including Yamabuki, had to admit, her mother's final choices were perfect.

But now that she was wrapped within the so-called twelve layers, *jūnihitoe*, Yamabuki began to feel overheated. She tried to console herself that the layers were a requirement of those of her station. Nonetheless, she began to sweat. She grew parched.

She turned her head slightly, catching Tomoko's gaze. *Mizu*, Yamabuki silently mouthed. *Water.*

Quickly Tomoko scurried away, and came back with a ladle, stretching out her arm. Rei pushed it away, chiding, "Away with that! What if you spilled it? You want to ruin what we're doing? Stain the kimono?"

Tomoko backed away, looking down, which did not please Yamabuki, who again thought to complain to Lady Taka. This was an unusually warm spring day, and Tomoko was only trying to help. But then Yamabuki again thought better of it. She would have to get used to it. After all, it was something every noble-woman endured. Elegant ladies rarely removed all their kimono layers—maybe only twice a year, when warm weather permitted bathing.

Besides, the preparations were far from over. There would be no complaining. Not today.

All at once, two of the nyōbō put protective towels across Yamabuki's kimono, for it was time for the face-color compounds, all to be applied in a precise manner and as custom dictated. In the meantime, two attendants took to brushing and oiling Yamabuki's hair. The locks had never even been trimmed, let alone cut. They remained long, silky, stunning, and raven black. But owing to her youth, they hardly fell as far as her waist. The handmaids whispered to console her. One day her hair might reach the floor, hopefully by the time she went looking for a husband.

Three of the nyōbō crowded in on Yamabuki. "Close your eyes," said the first as she started to powder Yamabuki's face with *oshiroi*, a finely ground rice-white facial foundation.

"Now you'll be as pale as a God," said a second handmaid who joined in the powdering.

"Open," said the third to Yamabuki.

Yamabuki, her eyes still closed, opened her mouth to ask *"Open what?"* only to feel the thrust of a small brush against her teeth and gums.

"Blech!" Yamabuki gasped as her tongue encountered a pungent paste. "It's foul!" Indeed it was, for it was a concoction of rust, stale saké vinegar, and the most horridly bitter ground nuts.

"It's just *haguro,*" one the nyōbō soothed.

"Pooh!" Yamabuki spat out more of the paste. "It's horrid. I'm not married. I don't have to blacken my teeth." She kept her eyes tightly shut as if it would make all the unpleasant tastes go away.

"Good we had the towels," one of the nyōbō said, for Yamabuki had spat the *nurude* paste over everything. Some of it even found its way to the floor, where one of the porters immediately dropped to her knees to wipe it up.

"The oshiroi is smeared," lamented a handmaid. Quickly another handmaid reapplied fresh powder.

"Take it away!" Yamabuki commanded, waving her hand imperiously.

Her mother interrupted sharply. "What's this? You forget yourself!"

Yamabuki looked up, suddenly contrite as her mother loomed over her. "I don't *want* to blacken my teeth."

Her mother was drawn. "You want everyone to think you have yellow teeth?"

"They aren't yellow," Yamabuki objected. "They're white as pearls. You said so yourself."

"Except when someone is wearing oshiroi. Everything else looks drab against white face powder."

"I am not married," Yamabuki sulked.

The nyōbō had gone blank faced, as they knew to do when mother and daughter were in this state of affairs with one another.

Lady Taka sighed deep. "Bring her that water," she commanded with a flourish of her hand.

Tomoko finally got close enough to deliver the graceful bamboo ladle. Yamabuki quaffed the water down in hardly more than one huge gulp.

"More!" Yamabuki rasped even before she finished it.

Her mother nodded, and in moments Tomoko returned with another ladleful. Yamabuki drank most of that down, too. At this, Yamabuki seemed to rally, and her mother said, "Everyone will be in white make-up today, even your father."

Yamabuki looked up from the water cup.

Her mother nodded. "And he's blackening his teeth, too, because it's in your honor. Yes?"

Yamabuki stopped scowling and nodded slowly and, resigned, thrust her chin forward, closed her eyes, curled back her lips, bared her teeth, and waited for the brush.

Finally came the fragrances—the extracts of flowers. It was said that, over time, the perfumes a woman chose would mingle with her other natural scents to permeate her costume, hair, and body. In combination, they would identify her as precisely as any of her features, so much so that a husband could distinguish amongst his wives even in the pitch darkness of a bedchamber. And, as Yamabuki was later led to understand, if a wife surreptitiously brought someone other than her own husband into her own bed, the next day the visitor was all but required to write poems to eternally glorify the mingling of these unique aromas—of course never mentioning the lady by name. That was revealed only through artful inference and subtle hints. Her personal scents. Her breath. The odor of decaying teeth was said to be especially sensual. Poetry.

In this aspect, Yamabuki did not share a poet's sensibilities. She found that the fine ladies, after a time, developed a certain stale pungency. Yamabuki found it hard to abide how older women began to reek, no matter how much perfume they applied. How could a man exalt *that* smell? But they did. It was said to drive men mad.

Her musings ended when her mother addressed her sharply.

"It's time."

Lady Taka, with a flourish of the hand, dismissed everyone, save for Yamabuki. In moments, the chamber, which had been filled with over thirty people, was now clean and quiet, its doors tightly shut—empty, save for mother and daughter.

Yamabuki stood where she had been left, clad in elegance. She knew her mother wanted her alone to say something. Would she tell Yamabuki that a husband had already been chosen for her and that's why she was having mogi? Was that why they insisted she blacken her teeth today?

Yamabuki gulped, and waited to hear her fate.

TWENTY-NINE

SAYONARA, MY DAUGHTER

LADY TAKA'S GAZE LINGERED on her daughter's perfectly made face. Despite spending half the day to make her even more beautiful, in her mother's eyes she was already perfection. There was no way in which nature could be improved upon. Lady Taka nodded to herself and whispered, "You are the most beautiful daughter a mother could ever wish to have, and you are so . . ." But she did not finish saying what was in her mind. Her daughter was not only beautiful, she was also bright, intelligent, and physically talented. Who would not want and cherish such a daughter!

Lady Taka was not one to readily lavish praise on her royal child who, she feared, would be inundated with nothing but praise—earned, unearned, or otherwise—until her ability to discern truth would wither out of a surfeit of blandishment.

She would resist telling the child how much she loved her. She would not reveal her own feelings, even to a daughter she was about to lose—especially to the daughter she was about to lose. Lady Taka would not impose her own sorrows onto her daughter on a day of such joy and import—a day after which Yamabuki would move to her own separate estate house along the west side of the Taka compound. Yamabuki was already burdened enough. Rarely was Yamabuki as temperamental as she had been when she had her teeth blackened.

At first, Lady Taka wore a warrior *mempo*—but not one of iron, though she, of course, had worn an iron-plate battle mask on any number of occasions. Today she wore a warrior's impassive expression, as impenetrable as any iron mask. As much as she might sympathize with her daughter, revealing her own sorrows in front of her would not be of help. Lady Taka would be strong for herself and, in so doing, would also be strong for her daughter.

And yet, Lady Taka realized that being a woman of iron, at this time, on this day, would be a mistake. She would be forgoing something inestimable. Lady Taka knew that she needed to say more to Yamabuki. There were last words that mother and child had to speak, at least in a formal way. Indeed, it was farewell—the truest, fullest, and deepest meaning of the word sayonara. It could not be all battle masks and iron wills, just so long as it did not excoriate Lady Taka's heart, for she kept that tightly wrapped. Not only did her husband not fully know her heart, she suspected she had never actually revealed it even to herself.

But there was no time to linger on thoughts of herself. That would come later, if ever. This was her daughter's day, and now was the time to think of Yamabuki, and only of her. Lady Taka said simply, "Today you enter womanhood and all that it means."

Yamabuki looked away. "Tomoko said something."

Lady Taka ever so slightly inclined an ear, indicating she was ready to listen. "What did Tomoko say?"

"She said there are whispers that I will be made the next daimyō. Could that possibly be true?"

Lady Taka breathed in. "Well," she said. This was the way she always started to say something which gave her pause. "As far as you becoming the next daimyō, it would only happen if there was no suitable match." Lady Taka sidestepped the physical requirements of being a warlord.

She saw too much of herself in Yamabuki and knew that her child's resolute side came from the Itō blood, which mother and daughter shared in their veins. She also saw in her the Taka blood of Yamabuki's father, which mother and daughter did not share with one another. Though the Taka were fierce warriors, wild in battle and grim of countenance, those of that clan harbored a latent sense of humor, which Yamabuki often displayed, and often at the most unusual times. In the extreme, it meant the Taka were quite capable of unpredictable turns that served them well in battle and in the Council chamber. Maybe troops *would* follow Yamabuki into battle.

Yamabuki started to ask a question, but she hardly had a chance as her mother continued. "You are young and beautiful. You know that, don't you? You'll have no difficulty finding a man, maybe a young heir who will be a daimyō in his own right, coming from a nearby land and with whom you will hopefully be in love."

"Boys are such oafs," Yamabuki sighed.

Lady Taka laughed softly. "Love's a waggish thing. It sneaks up on you. You might even see it coming and you think that you can brush it aside like a falling leaf, but when it comes, it disarms you and *you* become the leaf yourself, blown about by every whim of the wind."

"I asked some of the older girls about what to expect after mogi. What it felt like to be courted."

"Indeed? And what did they say?"

"They giggled."

"Giggled?" Lady Taka raised her brow.

Yamabuki reddened. "They said, why was I asking? They said I was still just a little girl and that I'm not interested in finding a husband or having children."

Lady Taka looked into Yamabuki's eyes. "Are you a little girl?"

Yamabuki hesitated, looking for a long moment, and shook her head.

Lady Taka said, "Your father and I would not have you go through mogi if we did not think you were ready." With a flick, she moved her hand dismissively. "Do you think being an adult is just about having children? About finding a husband?"

Yamabuki pondered before answering, "No."

"Never forget you are a daimyō's daughter. It's obvious that others seem to have forgotten—but then again, what can be expected of children, even ones who have gone through mogi? Even those with husbands." Lady Taka said, "This is a time of testing."

"I will do my best." Yamabuki looked plaintive. "I have worked very hard to memorize *The Tale of the Taka*."

Lady Taka warmed. "No. I did not mean that. It is not you who is being tested so much as you are testing everyone else. Who is standing by you?"

Yamabuki answered without hesitation. "You. Father. Lord Nakagawa. Tomoko. A few of the others."

"Yes." Her mother nodded. "Remember that in the future, when you will be in a high station. After today, you will find yourself surrounded by servile flatterers. When that time comes, recall where they were when you were still soaring up the side of the tall cliff, but not yet at the top." Lady Taka pursed her lips, her eyes dark as a hawk's. "Those girls who tittered"—Lady Taka laughed without the slightest mirth—"will still be trying to look as beautiful as they did on their wedding day, though they will never look so good again. You, on the other hand," she said with outstretched arms touching Yamabuki's shoulders, "are destined for great things." Lady Taka slipped her hand into her own kimono sleeve and pulled out the folded tessen. "Do I need to tell you what this is?"

Yamabuki shook her head. "No, mother. I know. It's your war fan."

Lady Taka's expression was tender. "And you know why a daimyō's wife carries a fan of iron instead of cloth or paper, yes?"

"Because she might be called on to lead troops into battle?" Yamabuki said with a small, unsure smile.

"It symbolizes her readiness to defend her castle whether her husband is there or not. This tessen was given to me by Mother before I left home to marry your father. It has been handed down through the line of Itō women going back at least ten generations, probably many more."

Yamabuki nodded.

Lady Taka stretched her arm out, holding the fan in front of Yamabuki. "Take it."

Yamabuki looked questioningly.

"I give it to you."

"Mother?" Yamabuki gasped, her eyes wide.

"It's yours now."

Yamabuki hesitated.

"Go on," her mother said warmly.

Yamabuki took the folded fan into her hands and gazed down at the silver metal tarnished slightly black with age. She eyed the intricate patterns of a leaf design etched into the surface. Not very deep. Not enough to weaken the web, but enough to catch the light. She had never been permitted to touch it before, and now it was hers. "It's so heavy," she said.

"Indeed it is heavy, just as a daimyō's wife's role is."

"I have no husband and no castle to defend."

"You may not have a husband. Not yet. But your castle is here at the Taka compound. And I know if we were under attack, you would not hesitate to lead our troops into battle. It's why you must commit *The Tale of the Taka* to memory. You carry that fan and know *The Tale of the Taka* so that you never forget who you are."

Leaving aside all her resolve to not reveal all that she really felt on this day, Lady Taka concluded, with tears welling up, "You are capable of much! Never forget that."

Yamabuki looked up, eyes questioning. "But if I should not? If I never marry . . . if I have to be the daimyō? A woman. Alone. What then?"

Lady Taka said, "Hush daughter. You will find someone. Of that I have no doubt. You will find happiness."

THIRTY

THE DOLL WITH A TEMPER

WHEN THE CHAMBER DOORS swept aside again, Lady Taka stepped out into the corridor and, accompanied by two of the eight handmaids who had waited just outside, disappeared into the corridor that led to the Great Audience Hall.

Yamabuki stepped into the hallway. She walked in as stately a manner as a child of twelve years could manage while wearing the heavy karaginumo. But no matter. The six remaining nyōbō of Lady Taka walked close by. The nyōbō formed around her like a guard, gently leading her forward. They all but ignored Tomoko, who followed Yamabuki's long, colorful kimono train, the *shitagasane*. As it slid across the floor, its silk hissed like far away ocean waves. The party made their way through the stuffy, sinuous halls where the scent of pine and bamboo-paneled walls mingled with the smell of dye and silk.

Yamabuki turned her head quickly, catching Tomoko's gaze.

"Look ahead or you might stumble," Rei admonished.

Yamabuki complied, but not before, through blackened teeth and crimson lips, she silently mouthed words to Tomoko: *Come beside me.*

Tomoko stepped to the edge of the hallway, trying to slip by, but with Lady Taka's handmaids on all sides, Tomoko found no way to get closer. It was as if there had been an unvoiced agreement amongst the nyōbō not to relinquish any space to the young handmaid, the one person in the party who had not whitened her face, nor blackened her teeth, nor reddened her lips or cheeks. The nyōbō actually seemed to take pleasure in peering down their noses at the out-of-place girl in their midst. So young, even younger than the not-yet-adult woman, Yamabuki.

As the party paused at the closed entry door panels to the Great Audience Hall, Tomoko still trailed. Again Yamabuki beckoned her forth. Tomoko started to press past Rei, but Rei shifted and, in what could only have been a deliberate move, subtle though it was, nudged Tomoko against the corridor wall.

"Stand aside, child!"

Yamabuki whirled around in her royal regalia. "Enough, Rei!" Yamabuki snapped. "*You* stand aside!" Yamabuki pushed Rei's shoulder, shoving her into two other nyōbō. Yamabuki's make-up did not hide her flashing temper.

Aghast, all six of her mother's attendants retreated a half step, which was remarkable given there was hardly any room to move anywhere in the corridor's confines.

Yamabuki seized Tomoko's arm and drew her alongside. "And she's no child! Not after today! She's my nyōbō! And when I become an adult, she becomes an adult!"

Though Yamabuki was not yet an adult, everyone knew she would be within the hour. And all knew, without having to be told, the daimyō's daughter had just made her first royal pronouncement. Whether Tomoko had her mogi or not, Yamabuki had proclaimed Tomoko an adult. The rest was mere formality and would happen soon enough.

Rei sputtered, looking down, trying to hide that she had started to glare back at the young princess.

Yamabuki remembered herself. She was supposed to be a great Lady, like her mother, who did not need to raise her voice. But Yamabuki was not finished with Rei either. Not yet.

Suddenly unseen hands slid the entry doors open. The midday light from the Great Audience Hall flooded the corridor where Yamabuki and the handmaids stood.

THIRTY-ONE

THUS THE FATE OF "THE TONGUE"

YAMABUKI WAS BLINDED BY the brightness coming from the Great Audience Hall. The sliding double walls all around the Hall's perimeter, which had been tightly shut since the previous autumn, were now pushed aside, revealing the open waters directly south, the Great Bay to the west, and the Windward Sea to the east, giving the illusion that the Hall was surrounded on three sides by ocean. Breakers could be heard crashing against the rocks below. The balmy, fresh, salty air filled the stuffy corridor.

As her eyes adjusted to the light, the dais, inside the Hall to the right, came into focus.

And it was as her mother had said: Lord Taka's face was rice-powder white. And his teeth were painted black. Dressed in his most formal robes, he stood on the dais, the broad, long-hanging sleeves of his formal burnt-orange kimono almost touching the floor. There were façades to be maintained and, like she, he was playing his part. This was a matter of state. Her mother serenely sat to the daimyō's left.

Yamabuki realized the slightly elevated dais provided a good view of the entry where Yamabuki stood, and she suddenly felt ashamed of how she had broken down back in the Chamber of Plum Blossoms.

Had they heard her shouting in the hall just now? Yet Lady Taka seemed unperturbed, and when she caught Yamabuki's eye, she gave her daughter a small warm hint of a smile. That smile meant everything to Yamabuki. Her mother did not tend to collect offenses. The earlier anguish over teeth blackening was all but forgotten.

"My Lady," Tomoko whispered, "your *kanzashi* has come loose." Quickly, she stepped between Yamabuki and Rei, reaching up to adjust Yamabuki's hair-band crown, straightening the hairpin that held the small decorative flowers in place.

Through the door, Yamabuki saw that the rest of the Hall, to the left, was filled with people. Her breath caught when she saw just how many had come to the mogi. The Hall, the most formal indoor place of gathering in the compound, was said to be large enough to "hold a village of a hundred," and if that were so, today it was at least a village and a half. And yet, though filled to capacity, the room remained hushed. While the Great Lord was standing on the dais, no one dared speak—not even in a whisper. It would have breached propriety.

From the entry, Yamabuki could see everyone, though those in the corridor's shadows could not be seen.

The retinue stood, shoulder to shoulder, so formally yet so festively dressed. The robes of the assembled were as varied and vivid as meadows of unimagined wildflowers. She looked down row after row.

The sea of white-powdered faces gave her the impression she was in the presence of the Gods and was about to cross onto The

High Plain of Heaven itself. She would walk amongst myriad snowy-white *kami*, all nearly translucent.

Yet in this sea of people, not Gods, she could name them all—a survival skill for a young princess who, on sight, had to know if someone was out of place, or if a stranger walked inside of the compound.

The main group stood by rank, at least a hundred counselors, warriors, and nobles, all facing front. First and foremost, her father's brother, Yamabuki's uncle, Prince Tachibana, stood in his regal trappings and make-up. To his immediate right, her cousin, Tachibana's son, Atsumichi, stood attired in the feminine clothing and hair that boys typically wore until their genpuku. Two black braids of hair rested on his shoulders. A gossamer veil hung over his face, though she could see his features easily.

Tachibana, who saw the daimyō looking toward the side entry, now turned his attention to Yamabuki. He let his eyes mirthfully meet hers.

She smiled back.

Atsumichi followed his father's gaze and saw Yamabuki. She offered her cousin a smile, too.

Suddenly, his tongue shot out at her from his all-white face— quick as a snake.

"I saw that!" Tomoko gasped.

Yamabuki wrinkled her nose. When Atsumichi's fleshy tongue darted out between unblackened teeth, it proved to Yamabuki that her mother was right: when details were left unattended, the outcome was hideous. Yellow teeth. Uncouth boy.

Her tone blasé, Yamabuki sniffed, "Alas, he's still merely a child." She stressed the word, turning it into a sarcastic hiss. "Thus the fate of 'The Tongue'!" Yamabuki innocently directed her eyes heavenward.

Tomoko giggled.

Little did the girls know at the time that the sobriquet would endure.

Rei cleared her throat. Obviously their conversation was not as discreet as the two girls had thought. Besides, this was not the way for the young princess to speak about a young prince, simpleton though he was.

Behind the main group, toward the back of the Hall, about twenty musicians sat, waiting quietly, their instruments at rest. Along the edge, crowding the walls opened to the air, were those related to the inner Court, mostly the wives and adult children, as well as some minor Court officials.

Then Yamabuki's eyes caught sight of someone she did not recognize. "Who's that?" she whispered to Tomoko. "A Shintō priest? Is there a blessing rite?"

Tomoko looked past Yamabuki and whispered, "He arrived this morning. Alone. Carrying a large bundle wrapped in silk."

The Taka compound's sonorous temple bell reverberated eight times. It was now the first quarter of the Hour of the Sheep.

Her father nodded imperceptibly to Yamabuki. It was time.

He sat, and the musicians started to play the staid High Court gagaku music. Her father seemed to love the compositions, but Yamabuki found them tedious, mournful, and at times even upsettingly sad. When the notes mingled with the sound of the ocean breakers, the music became haunting.

Yamabuki clutched the tessen. She had to remember, always, who she was.

"Go. Go," her mother's handmaids urged. "The music has started."

Yamabuki glanced over her shoulder. Eyes twinkling, the nyōbō nodded encouragingly. Tomoko flashed a broad smile.

The ceremony was underway.

"Wait! Wait!" one of them cried. "The *noshi*. The noshi." She tucked a small arrangement of *origami* into the kimono at the waist sash. "For luck."

"For luck," the others echoed.

"Who has the fan?" one of them suddenly gasped.

"I do," said Yamabuki, holding up the silver tessen.

Everyone's eyes lit up, even Rei's. They smiled in delight and bowed low.

She turned. Eyes ahead, she stepped through the portal.

THIRTY-TWO

THE DOLL WITH THE SWORD

A N EVEN DEEPER HUSH fell over the Great Audience Hall. The very wind held its breath. The only sounds were the music, the breakers, and the rustle of the silk of the long kimono train sliding across the floor with each step she took.

Using "the four stately footfalls" she had practiced, she moved toward the dais: Lead with the left foot, pull the back foot up in a dignified and deliberate way. The first three a shuffle, the fourth a slightly longer hesitation, almost a curtsy, and then raising back to full height. One-two-three, dip, and recover. Her hands down in front of her, helping to keep the kimono gathered, she held the tessen for all to see, its black silver a sharp contrast to the colorful costume. Everyone's eyes indeed fixed on it, if only fleetingly, in appreciation of its significance.

As a daimyō's daughter, she was used to formal courtesy, but when the entire clan moved as one, bowing in unison, everything—the entire room, the event, and everyone in it—took on a trance-like quality.

Is this what being a woman means?

In that single moment, she knew that everyone had moved her

to a different place in their minds. *Will they now start calling me by title? Taka-gimi.*

Yamabuki stopped before the dais, motionless for the briefest of instances. Then at once she went down to her knees, forehead to the floor, hands turned, palms flat with fingers pointing to the centerline in the Taka manner.

"*Tennō!*" she cried out in her young, feminine voice.

Formal greetings, bows, and acknowledgments were exchanged, after which she was permitted to kneel upright, seated on her heels, her instep, as always, flat against the floor—though, with all the thick chemises, she found it hard to feel the polished planking beneath.

The ceremony proceeded with the sipping of saké in observance of a new relationship, similar to that of a bride and groom at a wedding. Three black-lacquered bowls as elegant as any found in the City of the Moon were filled to the brim with milky-white liquid. Her parents drank first. Then she. They each took three sips. Then the cups were refilled. This cycle of three sips was repeated three times. For the moment, the drinking was confined to Lord Taka, Lady Taka, and Taka Yamabuki, though from attending the mogi of others she knew there would be plenty of saké drinking amongst the retinue after the ceremonies.

Yamabuki found this particular saké delicious and wished she could drink more.

The saké ceremony was followed by dull speeches and pointless pronouncements. During what seemed like never-ending banter, she went over the lines of the poem in her mind, reviewing several places where she always tripped. *The Tale of the Taka* was not just long, it was intricate and convoluted. She would proclaim every ancestor, name every lofty individual, and cite every exciting exploit and daring deed of the clan and its vassals. And it was not just that. The years in which the events took place were recounted by reigns and eras: the fifth year of some emperor or other, followed by two years of the next emperor, followed by several years of the third emperor's era, and so on.

It was not as if the poem was unknown—the retinue had sung it many times, but always in unison, for everyone more or less knew it by heart and loved it—but today her solo voice would have to fill the entire Hall, and fill it flawlessly, for if she tripped but once, everyone would know it, and this would not reflect well.

Two months earlier, she had protested to her mother that boys at their genpuku did not have to sing *The Tale of the Taka*, only girls did for mogi. Lady Taka had answered that boys did not take husbands, only girls did, and so if a husband wanted to be entertained with a lovely story, it was up to a wife to sing to him and soothe him. Yamabuki said this was stupid. There were plenty of musicians and singers in the compound to do all the required singing and soothing. Why should a wife have to do this? Yamabuki doubted she would ever want or require a husband, especially if she had to spend her days singing and soothing.

Lady Taka was not amused. In a sharp tone, she informed her daughter that she herself had learned *The Tale of the Taka* as an adult in order to marry Lord Taka, and if she could do it, Yamabuki would learn it, too. There would be no debate on this point. Yamabuki was commanded to sing and sing she would, no matter what her fanciful ideas about marriage were. But Yamabuki had seen the worry in her mother's eyes.

A Taka compound temple bell now sounded out. The Second

Half of the Hour of the Sheep had come. Yamabuki's stomach churned. She tried not to let her nervousness show. She expected that it would take until the Hour of the Monkey to complete *The Tale of the Taka*; she had timed it out again and again with Tomoko, who had snuck an unwieldy water-clock into Yamabuki's chambers to time the rehearsals.

To accompany Yamabuki, a musician named Fusa-ichi moved forward with his *kōjin-biwa*. He took his appointed place, just behind her and to the right. He cleared his throat—a signal to Yamabuki. They had never rehearsed together, for he was not of her class. *What a stupid distinction*, she thought to herself. *We've never even spoken.*

There was another a moment of silence. Yamabuki took a deep breath.

Fusa-ichi then plucked the first note. In her high, young voice, she began to sing,

> *In the place where the shining orb touches the People of the Sun*
> *As always, and in ancient times, before any place else,*
> *The Sun Goddess shined Her first light on the land of the Great Bay*
> *To grace the people called the Taka.*
>
> *When man's time dawned, Taka ancestor Great-Hawk-Fire-Wind-Seeker drew his bow*
> *Shooting a single stone arrow into the High Plain over the Autumn Creek Land.*
> *Weeping-Maiden-of-the-Milky-River-of-Stars then caught the arrow*
> *She threw down the first grains of rice like tears from Heaven.*

Yamabuki directed her attention to the dais, and since everyone else was behind her, she more or less ended up singing only to her parents, which made it both easier and more difficult to perform. She noticed every now and then that her mother nodded ever so slightly in approval, or perhaps in encouragement, at the parts where Yamabuki had encountered difficulty during practice.

When she finished, there was a murmur within the Hall. She knew she had done well, for she could see relief in the corners of her mother's eyes. Yet for Yamabuki, the last half of the Hour of the Sheep had passed quickly. Maybe too quickly. Had she sung too fast? No. She finished exactly on time, for just then the temple bell tolled seven times—the first quarter of the Hour of the Monkey. The sun already blazed over the western sea, and now began the last span of the afternoon before the sky took on its orange hues.

Yamabuki had been led to believe that her singing of *The Tale of the Taka* would conclude the rite, but then two of her father's largest and toughest bodyguards, Etsu and Jun, strode toward the dais. She almost did not recognize them in their finery, for the idea that they would wear anything but their armor had never entered her mind; but there they stood: Etsu in dark-blue silk, Jun in gold.

Etsu held a long wooden box, which he solemnly brought before her father. The Hall stirred. In that one moment, Lord Taka was the focus of everything—warlord and daimyō.

All at once, her mother's face went blank. Even Yamabuki, for all her knowledge of her mother's moods, was not sure what might be going through her mother's mind.

Her father's eyes darted toward Yamabuki. He looked intently. She knew that look. He was up to something, and it involved her.

On one knee, Jun took the box from Etsu and stretched out his arms, cradling it as if he were presenting a newborn to the Great Lord. Etsu pulled the lid back. Her father reached in, lifting out a long, dark drawstring sack. The bodyguards quickly undid the string, and pulled the cloth away at the top to reveal a sword hilt wrapped in black leather and cobalt-blue silk.

"Yukiyasu." Her father called out but this single name.

She heard shifting behind her and sensed movement. She permitted herself a fleeting glance over her shoulder.

The Shintō priest that Tomoko had identified earlier was making his way toward the dais, bowing without exactly kowtowing. As he approached, she noticed that his hat was actually not that of a priest at all, but of a similar style—that of a craftsman. The man was old, wiry, white-haired, with wrinkled skin and age-pouted lips, but oh the eyes! Like a bird of prey.

As protocol would have it, he stopped just back of Yamabuki.

"Swordsmith Yukiyasu has brought his skill," Lord Taka began as he pulled the scabbard from the sack, the latter which he tossed aside. The *saya* bore the Taka crossed-feathers mon, the lacquer gleaming even in the indirect afternoon light within the Hall. Her father's eyes danced.

When she glanced at her mother, she saw that the polite smile painted on her face did not match the ever-growing darkness in her eyes.

Lord Taka called Yamabuki forward. She rose on her arches—which, despite the years of practice sitting in this position, were numb. She stood, and with slow, stately steps approached the dais.

The man in the Shintō garb, likely the selfsame Yukiyasu, walked several steps behind her. She continued up onto the dais, but the smith stopped well back, coming no further than the spot Yamabuki had vacated. He was turned so that he mostly faced forward, but also so that he could look back at the retinue.

Yamabuki, standing on the dais, could see everyone. And everyone was looking at her. She looked to her left, toward the side entry. The door was still partially open and shadowy, but Tomoko stepped forward from among the nyōbō, far enough to be in the light. Only someone on the dais could see her. Yamabuki gave a slight smile meant only for Tomoko. Those in the Hall likely thought that Yamabuki was solemnly smiling at the retinue, or at least at the sword, and so everyone smiled back, equally formally. All except Tomoko, who beamed.

"Please accept this humble sword," Yukiyasu said, his voice soft as he bowed. He remained motionless, holding the bow as ritual demanded.

It was a matter of protocol that a sword could not go directly from a mere smith's hands to those of a Lord. Only one of the inner circle was permitted to hand a weapon to someone of her father's rank. No commoner, whatever the reason, not even the one who created it, was permitted to draw a blade anywhere near a warlord.

"Come." The daimyō held out the saya to Yamabuki.

She looked at him expectantly, taking a step closer to stand right beside him.

"Take it," he said in a whisper loud enough to be heard throughout the Hall.

Her right hand seized the scabbard, which was almost as thick in her fist.

He nodded. "Show us," he hissed to her with a curled lip, both terrible and humorous in his expression.

With her left hand, she tugged on the hilt. For the first time ever, she heard the characteristic hiss her blade made that in years to come would be commonplace to her. She continued pulling until the steel, in all its glimmering magnificence, was free.

The retinue, almost as one, grunted in approval, "Ha!"

"It's *heavy*," Yamabuki muttered.

"Swordsmith Yukiyasu," Lord Taka said, "tell us about this blade."

There was a long silence filled only by the crash of the breakers against the rocky shores.

"Tennō!" Yukiyasu began, lifting his head from the long bow. If there was ever any doubt about the swordsmith being a priest, such doubts were dispelled. Like a prophet's, Yukiyasu's voice grew mighty as it carried throughout the Great Audience Hall. It rose to the high rafters and drowned out the sounds of the ocean. "The sword Taka-gimi holds is the best I have ever made."

He is *calling me by that title—Taka Princess.* Yamabuki found the title jarring.

Yukiyasu shifted his attention straight to the dais and addressed the daimyō and Yamabuki in a most solemn manner, again his eyes mysterious and other-worldly. "Swords are unyielding vessels which carry a warrior's spirit within. In making a sword, a master must combine the five elements of the universe, and it is their interwoven and combined expression that Taka-gimi now holds."

Yamabuki did not start this time as Yukiyasu referred to her by the lofty title. She smiled inwardly. She was beginning to get used to it, at least when Yukiyasu said it.

The swordsmith continued his speech, in which he told of how—in general terms, never giving away his secret techniques—he had made the finest sword ever. He described its construction, emphasizing its many parts. The tip alone had three identifiable sections, each with specialized names.

Yamabuki found this fascinating, as did the warlord's personal retinue, but she could see that the swordsmith's speech, stentorian though it was, was lost on those who did not carry swords. They strove to hide the fact that they were quickly losing interest and becoming bored—all, that is, except Tomoko, who hung onto every word.

Yukiyasu, as if he were saving the best for last, invited Takagimi-Yamabuki to look at the temper line—a distinctive pattern burnt into the steel, running just above the cutting edge. Yukiyasu said her sword carried the *sanban-sugi-zai nami*, the three-cedar-wood-zigzag pattern.

Lord Taka, with a flicking movement of his hand, had Yamabuki lift the blade high. As one, the retinue responded with another manly grunt, "Ha!"

Her father whispered, hardly moving his lips, "Is this not worthwhile? One day, after I am gone, you may need to lead the Taka into battle. Starting tomorrow, I shall personally take over your fencing instruction."

She shot him a look.

He continued so only she could hear, "Nakagawa will also continue teaching you as before." He looked into her eyes with an intensity she had never seen, and a grin he might only wear in battle. "Something you and I should have started a long time ago." He glanced at the retinue and said, "Go on. Show them." He thrust his chin toward her. "You are a warrior now"—he paused—"and my daughter."

Holding the blade in her left hand, she reached with her right into her sleeve and pulled out the tessen, and with a snap of the wrist opened the war fan. Though it was the first time she had ever performed the act, it opened with the same snapping sound that her mother could make it produce.

She lifted blade and tessen over her head.

The assembled stirred in surprise. They had seen swords lifted and they had seen tessen lifted, but Taka Yamabuki lifted both.

THIRTY-THREE

WOMEN'S ARMOR

YAMABUKI BLINKED, returning from her reminiscence of mogi all those years before. Her brush had not touched the parchment. Suddenly she no longer had any inclination to write. Maybe there was too much to say and nowhere to begin. She put her brush down on the ink stone. She removed her saké bottle from the saddle bag and pulled the stopper. *Yes. Still empty.* She laughed at herself, though it was not the least bit funny, nor did she feel the least bit sated, nor did she feel even faintly drunk from the kushi. If anything, it made her feel ill. It was either the fermented barley or the buri she had eaten that afternoon.

She recalled the Ōe clan crest—orange with the single upright arrow feather—which she had seen worn by the *sakimori* who laughingly killed Blue Rice, a man who had befriended her. Blue Rice, whose companionship she grew to enjoy during the crossing of the Barrier Strait. There was an ancient saying: *In but a moment, you can make a friend for life.*

Though she wanted some saké, she did not regret having poured a third of her canteen onto the cenotaph as an offering—*Omiki* to the Gods. It was the senseless death that offended her, the ease with which low-ranking guards could murder someone with impunity. All under the guise of protecting Nagato Prefecture.

No longer in Ō-Utsumi, here her rank meant little when it came to local matters. She was just another forgettable warrior making her way to the capital.

Still, to end a day like this, going to bed hungry, did not at all seem fitting. Perhaps the saké house was the right destination after all, if only to drink and maybe to forget.

Did she need to record everything in her pillow book tonight? Would she ever forget? Could she ever forget? Doubtful.

She put her writing implements aside and found the small polished steel mirror that she kept within a soft cloth sack in her saddlebags. The brazier light that Mari left proved sufficient to illuminate Yamabuki's face.

She studied the cut to her left cheek. The nick started just below her eye. *Another gash.* Like the one to her corselet. An imperfection. She leaned into the mirror. The eye closest to the cut gazed back. The lesion no longer oozed sap. Already a small scab had started to fix itself into place. Taro had said both her face and her armor would return to their former appearance without the slightest trace. She hoped he was right. Time would tell.

In the meantime, she would be forced to conceal this flaw behind another kind of armor—the armor employed by women in battles that did not involve the sword.

Yamabuki's mother had spoken of Rei's pockmarked face and what that meant to a young woman looking for a husband. Apart from Rei, all of Rei's family had died when the pox struck, leaving Rei a veritable orphan. There was no one to arrange a marriage for Rei and no title or property to make the match more attractive.

There was a saying: *What beauty could not supply, money could buy.* Marred for life, without a dowry, Rei likely would never marry someone of the class into which she was born, that is if she married at all.

Would the facial wound relegate Yamabuki to a similar fate? She knew that, with her father as daimyō, she would marry well, irrespective of a scar. What money would buy! Yamabuki had seen that some rather unattractive women had married quite well, provided they were of sufficient rank, for what was rank but a form of wealth?

Still, every woman of the Court had to "make an effort," as her mother always reminded her.

She decided to stop thinking about that. She had entered a world which few women had dared enter. *How did mother ever get through it—entering musha shugyō a whole year younger than me?* She thought of the idle pastimes and the innocence of the court games that girls and boys played. Life outside the compound was indeed harsh and cruel. No wonder saké was such a welcome relief.

But getting saké meant that she would have to venture out into the town.

What to do about her still-raw facial scar? Make-up would cover it, but if she were to wear make-up, would she not be laughed at? The common people did not wear make-up. Almost nobody did. They did not pluck their brows and wear them in *chō* style—butterflies. Most of the women had those awful caterpillar brows, never to be butterflies—the kind the young women of the Taka Court would laugh about.

She looked in the mirror again. Scar or make-up, either way, she would stand out. The third alternative was to forgo the saké.

"Humph." After today, nothing could keep her from a good flask—maybe two or three.

It had been five years since mogi and she no longer needed a corps of nyōbō to apply her make-up. She could do it without Tomoko's help. Of course she could, almost without thinking.

She opened the small, black-lacquered box filled with the familiar oshiroi. Taking a small but wide brush, she applied the white rice powder to her cheeks, forehead all the way down and on past her chin. The bristles stung when they insulted the cut, but the powder hid the wound rather well.

Next, above her now-whitened natural eyebrows, she painted chō, higher than her actual browline. She ever so slightly touched *benibana*—ruby-red dye—to her cheeks, but then, generously in thickness but sparingly in circumference, applied the color to her lips to make them look smaller but more intense.

To her hardwood hairbrush she added a skosh of walnut oil— the same kind that she had used as a child to keep her wooden practice sword from cracking, except that this oil was also scented with a tinge of nutmeg. She brushed the locks, working its teeth into the hair, pulling down on the long tresses. She guided each stroke gently and carefully, passing from the crown to the ends. Any captured stray hairs were relegated to the irori. There the strands crackled, sputtered, and flared as the whitish-orange and reddish-blue flames consumed them.

She laughed at herself.

I am *superstitious after all. Do I* really *think someone wishes to work magic on me?*

Finally she tied a small streamer ribbon, cream in color, at the back of her head to keep the locks off her face—just to make sure her peripheral vision was unobstructed. *Hm. It complements the kimono's orange.*

She stuffed Tiger Cub through her sash. She took a last look in the mirror. She was ready.

She placed the three scrolls, along with a tantō, into her kimono sleeve.

Forgoing the dainty footwear that would otherwise be required of someone dressed in the kind of finery which she wore, she followed Mari's advice and put on her warm, silk-lined boots. *It doesn't matter, they won't show.*

She pushed the door aside. It seemed Mari had already removed the dirt from the rails, for the panel quietly and easily slid open. She stepped into the dark evening, closing the heavy door soundlessly behind her.

She walked carrying a single brazier torch. Five bell strikes reverberated through Minezaki. Shokō, the First Watch, fifth hour, Hour of the Dog. It was the third night of Kokuu, the solar stem of the Grain Rain. The time when birds mate.

THIRTY-FOUR

THE GENTIAN SAMURAI

THICK CLOUDS ROLLED OVER the full moon, turning the sky all but black. She walked along the trail from Ledge Road into town. A biting mountain wind wailed up, rustling the barely leafing trees. It blew against her kimono hem and tried to snuff out the flickering brazier. The orange kimono proved surprisingly warm, but nevertheless Yamabuki still felt enough of the cold to shiver.

Soon she arrived at the head of the main street. It was deserted. There was hardly a street torch anywhere. *How squalid.*

A forsaken brazier sputtered in front of the building with the rustic, dark-green banner with the saké calligraphy. Light seeped from cracks in the entry door and windows of the establishment. The two yahochi were long gone. Perhaps they were inside. What did she care? Her face stinging with the cold, she moved gingerly to the door and entered.

The place was almost as deserted as the street. Dim, lit only by five braziers. One attendant—wiry, with silver hair and a well-worn white-and-brown-striped kimono—mumbled something she was intended to overhear, but not quite, something about it not being worth the coal to light and wood to heat the place with so few customers. The only customer was a man of her years seated by himself at a small table. His only company was an earthen saké flask. His tachi sword, in its scabbard, stood leaned up against the wall within easy reach. The sword sheath displayed the same gentian-flower-and-bamboo-leaf clan crest as she had seen at Taro's shop.

So. That's him.

He glanced toward her.

She met his eyes briefly in self-assurance, not in challenge. Even though she was dressed as anything but a warrior, she returned the gaze of confidence that samurai exchange.

He shot back a small smile—something not done among samurai. For only the briefest of moments, his eyes said something more, a hint of comprehension from him. But comprehension of what? His eyes flickered innocently. No. Something more there than plain innocence. And just as quickly, the two strangers looked away as she seated herself.

She chose a spot some distance across the room, her back to a wall where she could see who entered and who left through the main or side doorways. She figured that in a town like this, with the riff-raff that passed through, anyone with any experience would sit strategically.

She put Tiger Cub—still in its dark-green scabbard, its Taka insignia face down—on the table next to her and within easy reach.

"Saké House Man," she called out. "A flask of your best saké."

The Gentian Samurai chuntered, "There's no best. It's all the same saké." His voice was young, smooth, manly, yet with a silk-like quality. She immediately detected a dialect. The years she had spent living in the capital had developed her ear for accents, since they revealed things about people. His seemed to be the open accent of the western part of the central mountains: the Jōmō district. It also had traces of High Court speech.

She again, though circumspectly, looked in his direction, and noticed that he, too, sat strategically so that he could keep eyes on the doors. He seemed handsome enough, just as Kōno had said. Like many a young man, he was too young to have yet developed a beard or moustache, though he had an impressive mane of hair that hung far down his back and which he had bunched with a ribbon at the base of his scalp.

Hm. Almost as long as mine. He's pretty, too, enough so that a girl might envy him.

The wiry attendant ambled over with the flask she had ordered and with a thump set the bottle down in front of her.

"A copper," he muttered as if put-upon by having to serve her at all. "In advance," he added sullenly.

Yamabuki's eyes flashed darkly. "A bowl . . . ?" she hissed.

"Humph," he grumbled, retrieving the untouched saké bottle from the table, and then walked to the back of the shop, returning with the same bottle and a slightly chipped but clean-looking saké cup-bowl. He placed both before her.

With a flick of her thumb, she flipped him the asked-for coin, which the man was a little too slow in catching, fumbling, almost intercepting it but not quite. It clinked somewhere in the dark. The proprietor looked around in the dim light.

"Open your eyes. It's at your feet, if it's worth stooping for," she said peevishly.

He grunted as he bent down, picking the coin that had glanced off his instep.

The Gentian Warrior stared away at nothing in particular, acting as if he had missed the whole exchange, though he seemed to be smiling with slight amusement. She also noticed he drank without the nicety of a cup, straight out of the bottle. What manner of place was this? Of course she knew the answer. A place with yahochi.

The Gentian Samurai, innocent though he might look, was probably hoping for a tryst. Since she carried a medium sword, it would be plain to anyone that she was not there for anything else but drinking. He likely knew not to bother her.

She went back to disregarding him and took her first taste of the saké. *Dreadful!*

She must have grimaced, for the Gentian Samurai muttered, "Wait 'til you go further into the mountains. The saké's even worse."

Worse? She paused to consider. Of course it would be worse. Why would she be surprised?

Still in no mood for conversation, Yamabuki continued to pretend not to hear. All she desired was to be alone with her thoughts and to drink the saké, even if it was second rate. Third rate.

When she was on her third bottle, an odd thought crossed her mind: third-rate saké tasted better by the third bottle.

She looked in the samurai's direction again, hoping their eyes would meet a second time.

Commoners were excluded from the Taka compound. No commoner, thus, could look at a High Born person, especially a female. On the road, women did not hide behind veils and screens, so there was more eye contact. But she was traveling as a buké, and so far most commoners had avoided looking directly at her.

Now in her commoner's kimono, she recollected some of the advice her mother had offered her: If you are interested in a man, meet his eyes twice over the course of the evening, and only twice. After that, you will find out if he is interested.

But he did not meet her eyes. He was listening intently. He had heard something outside.

Then she heard it, too.

THIRTY-FIVE

TELL THEM ABOUT THE ROBBERS

A BLAST OF AIR blew in the night's chill when the entry door opened. Noisy and excited voices accompanied the wind. They belonged to five men who more or less at once barged in from the street. They were dressed in dark, nearly black, tunics complete with the insignia of the Ōe clan.

Though Yamabuki looked only from the corners of her eyes, at once she recognized that they were the very same sakimori border guards she had encountered earlier in the day—the very same ones who stood by as Blue Rice died. Their leader, Misaki, who did the actual killing, was not among them now. Of course not. Misaki was a lieutenant, and these cretins were dogs—soldiers, if they could even be called that—who did as they were told and who gave men like Misaki someone to order around and domineer.

Their drinking was already well advanced.

"It's cold out there."

"We need some saké."

"You're always slow, Unagi. Bring it fast this time."

"Long march. Our feet are tired."

"Throw some more wood on the fire."

"Wood?" the proprietor growled. "Wood's expensive!"

"Ha!" one of then scoffed. "We know it was you who stole the town sign, Unagi."

"Huh?" the proprietor gasped. "Not me!" he sniffed.

"Throw some wood on the fire, or we'll arrest you for taking the sign."

The proprietor seethed, but complied. The men settled around a table in the middle of the room.

"And while you're at it, bring us saké. We want *five* bottles!"

The last time Yamabuki saw them, they carried polearms. Now it seemed that they had exchanged them for short swords.

Will they recognize me? It was doubtful they would. She had been wearing full battle armor cap-à-pie at the time. Indeed, they had not looked closely at her.

For the moment, at least, they were more focused on getting their wine than noticing a woman with a sword who was sitting toward the back in half shadow.

"Unagi!" one of them insisted as though he were noble. At that, the proprietor, his face even more dour than before, walked to their table. He glowered.

Unagi, eh? Eel, she thought to herself. *Is that his real name or yet another insult?*

The men proceeded to boisterously speak a lot of nonsense which she found about as eloquent as dogs barking. She only took notice when one of them shouted out, "Unagi? Did you hear about the robbery and murder on the North Road at Akamagaseki?"

Unagi grunted. Either he had not heard or was not interested— probably both.

"We were the first ones there," one of them boasted, as if they had done something special. "They killed two unarmed monks," the guard continued. "An Ōuchi samurai tried to help, but the robbers killed him, too!"

Yamabuki looked down at her cup, though her ears perked.

One of the guards, the one who seemed to have taken on the role of storyteller, turned toward the Gentian Samurai. "What do you think of that! The dead samurai was very famous, too. Everyone knew him," he boomed. He screwed his face, trying to remember something. "What was his name again?"

"Shima," one of his fellows called out.

Shima, the others repeated.

"Shima Sa-me," one of them added.

"Right! Shima Sa-me. A man with a sword twice as long as any man would dare carry."

"A nodachi—two sword-lengths long."

"And heavy," said another of the number.

"He was the fencing master to the Ōuchi clan."

"Pah!" one of them grunted, dismissing the Ōuchi, the Ōe's sometime enemy.

"I heard he was told to leave by the new Ōuchi daimyō."

"His teaching was too harsh," one of them laughed with contempt.

"Tell them about the robbers," urged the third.

"Emptied their money pouches—turned them inside out. Left the bodies to rot in the road. Can you believe the heartlessness of some people? Killing holy men. Young and innocent ones at that."

All the other sakimori grunted in agreement.

First on the scene? Not if the dead were robbed. Of course, these men might have done the robbing themselves. They certainly were spending money quickly.

"We saw the three of them headed up the North Road more or less together," the first guard said to Unagi, who kept going on about his business, all but ignoring them.

"The fabric merchants and the Taka samurai weren't bothered."

"And that Taka girl with the fancy horse was lucky. She didn't get mixed up in it."

"The girl?"

One of them laughed wickedly. The others joined in.

"She probably rode away. She was mounted."

"I'd mount her!" another chuckled and the table erupted in lewd sounds. One of the others made mocking womanly gasps. His imitation was not meant to be accurate and thus the men chuckled all the harder.

"I can't imagine riding a woman wrapped in all that iron."

"Take all that fancy armor off and it's all the same," said the first man.

The others laughed uproariously.

Yamabuki, eyes slits, looked down, staring into her bowl. She slowly poured the last of her third flask into her cup. She motioned for Unagi to bring her another. No sooner was the fourth flask sitting on her table than, grinning ear to ear, the first of the sakimori approached her. She looked up, noticing he ambled unsteadily. *Can't hold his wine.*

"You're new to Minezaki, eh? Working for Kōno, I see." He gestured toward her kimono. "You stay here for long, you'll get to know us. Everyone knows us, right!" He turned to look back at his fellows and guffawed. They joined in with merry agreement. "Yes. Get to know us well. Yes?"

She did not answer. Her face showing no expression, she lifted her gaze and met his bloodshot eyes straight on. The man had the eyes of a fool.

She looked back at her cup.

"Why don't you smile, Saké House Girl?"

Saké House Girl, is it? She did not look up. "Why do you care?" she muttered.

"A girl such as yourself. Alone. I'll tell you what. We'll buy you saké—all the saké you want and then maybe we can *all* have some fun?"

She looked up and shook her head slowly, and looked back down at her cup. "I buy my own saké."

"Ha! Lots of money, eh? Must have been a pretty good night for you so far. Must have had a lot of *it*. But we can give you more." He guffawed again, and then regained his composure. "Come join me and my friends," he said through smiling teeth.

"I am planted where I am," she answered in a whisper through clamped teeth.

"Not without *this*," he laughed drunkenly and reached for her saké bottle.

His hand was almost to the bottle's neck when suddenly Tiger Cub's scabbard came to rest on top of his wrist—not hard, but firm.

Her expression stone, she said, "That does *not* belong to you."

The man's mirth instantly evaporated. His eyes flashed—a mixture of mostly surprise and a bit of anger at the supposed affront.

It was only an instant, but she recalled the keen eyes of Shima, Akibō, and Iebō—men who had killed. Expressions that gave away nothing during combat. This dog's eyes were nothing like that even as he tried to appear cross with her.

He might have walked away at that point—though probably not—were it not for his fellows who started to chuckle and make noises. He had now lost face and lost it to a woman no less. His jaw set. His mouth drew into a line. His eyes darted. He jerked his hand out from under the scabbard and again reached for the neck of the flask.

Before his fingers could seize it, she rapped his knuckles with the scabbard.

He let out a yowl as he took a half step back, waving his arm to shake off the stinging. His disbelief hardened into anger. "Yahochi!" He spat the word.

"You *dare* call me that!" she snarled.

He started to repeat the insult. "Yaho—" only he could not finish as her scabbard squarely landed against the side of his jaw. He wobbled and fell to the floor, where he lay without moving.

A hush descended over the room. Unagi looked aghast. The Gentian Samurai looked quite amused.

Her fourth saké bottle lay on its side. The only sound now was the sound of the saké escaping to the floor. *Blub-blub-blub.*

"Humph. You spilled my saké," she said softly with annoyance.

The remaining four sakimori stood up one by one. Faces twisted. Sneering.

"You've *killed* him!" snapped the one closest to Yamabuki.

"Hardly. Look closer," she said dryly.

Not satisfied, one of the guard went for his sword hilt.

Yamabuki bolted up from the bench and stepped toward him, and before he could pull his weapon, she delivered a solid blow with her scabbard to the wrist of his sword hand. The sound of the breaking bone filled the room. It sickened everyone, even her.

He screamed, "My wrist!"

The remaining three men looked to one another, obviously uncertain as to what they should do next.

One of them, who showed more anger than sense, started toward her. He also went for his sword. As he did, his body turned slightly from right to left, whereupon Yamabuki's scabbard found his right collarbone.

Another cracking sound. Another shriek.

The two screaming, injured men staggered toward the door of the saké house, leaving two men standing, frozen, the fifth unconscious on the floor.

"Get your friend and get out of here," she growled.

They quickly bowed to her, lifted their unconscious compatriot's shoulders, and hurried on, dragging him out the door, his heels scraping along the boards behind them.

"Too much saké and too much tongue," she muttered. "They could not have picked a *worse* day."

She looked over at the Gentian Samurai, who had sat motionless with the same amused smile frozen on his lips, but now, in addition, his eyes twinkled. He lifted his saké flask up as if in salute.

"Well," she said aloud. "Looks like those fellows left their saké unfinished. And they ruined my meditation." She stepped toward the now empty table with its five saké bottles. "I noticed that this one's full," she said out loud to no one in particular as she made a slight gesture toward her mouth with her left forefinger and grimaced. "I think his mouth did not touch it. I shall have to take my musing elsewhere."

Unagi blanched, bowed quickly, but said nothing.

The Gentian Samurai whispered softly in the tongue of the Sòng Dynasty,

The scent of saké.
Jade cups.
Amber light.

Yamabuki looked directly at him, smiling darkly. *Educated. More than just a pretty face with a sword.* She finished the poem in the language of the Autumn Creek Land.

The attendant plies us with drink.
So that we can forget home.

She picked up the bottle in question, took a deep drink, set it back down, and walked into the street, where it was colder and darker, if that was possible, than when she had arrived. Brazier in one hand, she started for the armory.

Footsteps approached quickly from behind.

The sakimori? They haven't had enough?

She slipped her hand toward Tiger Cub's hilt.

"Ha! Broken Armor!" she heard the Gentian Samurai's cry. "Wait!"

Thirty-Six
WANT TO GET DRUNKER?

YAMABUKI LOOKED OVER HER shoulder. The five sakimori hobbled away in the opposite direction. The Gentian Samurai followed her at least ten paces behind.

"Samurai-sama?" The Gentian Samurai approached her.

Am I going to have trouble with this one, too?

Her hand crept even closer to the short sword's hilt.

"Please stop so that I do not look like a Sòng Dynasty wife following several paces behind her husband."

She turned fully to look at him.

For the first time, they were face-to-face and not just exchanging fleeting glances. He laughed good-naturedly. The single street torch flickered in the almost totally dark night, its light glistening against his long black hair and shining teeth.

A cold gust of mountain wind kicked up the dust, nearly putting out the torch. She lifted her sword hand to shield the feeble flame of her own lamp.

"It's blowing down through the pass," the Gentian Samurai ventured. "We could get snow."

She nodded in agreement.

"You want to drink more saké so we can forget home?" he asked. She inclined her head, questioning.

"Like the poem you finished back there," he said.

"You know the language of the people of the Yellow River Delta?"

"Ha-ha," he laughed. "It's the only poem I know. Want to get drunker?"

"Not with that saké."

"That place was not so good, was it? Putrid saké."

"It seems it's the only place," she said.

"The House of Red Banners has saké."

She cast a sideways glance. "Red Banners?"

"Hai. The best saké in this town. It's right there," he said, pointing no more than three doors away down a short alley.

"It doesn't *say* saké," she said in a low tone.

"That's why it's the best. Not available to the commoners. Come."

"Why should I come with you?" She studied him.

"If for nothing else, then the saké." He dropped the grin and spoke quietly, "Because I suspect you might like to talk to someone other than oafs. Maybe someone who might know a bit about what you have gone through."

"And pray tell, what do you know what I have gone through?"

He smiled crookedly. "It was good that you came to the saké house. Not much of anything to do in this town anyway. You ran off five men without ever drawing your blade. Besting five is something to be remembered."

"They were drunk."

"So were you." When she darkened, he quickly added, "and so

am I. Would you like to come inside? I am telling the truth. The saké's good."

"And what would happen should I get drunk with you?"

"Whatever you like."

"What if it's nothing."

"Then nothing it shall be."

She looked toward the small house. The red banners fluttered in the cold night wind.

He said, "We have both been through much the same. I saw your armor at Kōno's. That cut tells a story."

"Ah, a diviner."

"No," he went on thoughtfully, "but I did hear the sakimori's accounts of a robbery, none of which I believe. Someone robbing monks? Since when do robbers want something of monks? And if these robbers were so skilled that they killed a sword master, why did they leave swords and armor. Old Kōno there would have given them something in trade. And it was not just because the sakimori happened onto the scene and the robbers ran off." He lowered his voice. "You know what I think? I think those three dead men on that road had decided, for whatever reason, to take on someone else—a fourth person. And I also think that they underestimated their opponent and ended up like cormorants, unable to swallow what was in their throats." He looked at her impassively. "I think they picked a fight and they lost. Does that sound logical to you?"

Yamabuki said nothing.

"Ever kill a man?" he asked quietly.

She did not answer, her eyes growing dark, meeting his.

"I can see you have," he said. "And it was not luck that you survived. It was skill. Great skill. Nodachi? I've never had to face that." He nodded slowly.

The wind picked up. The tall red banners began to flap harder.

"Mountain winds." He sniffed. "It will get colder tonight, but it's warm inside."

Finally, she said softly, "I will drink saké with you." She looked at him long and hard. "That is, if you have a clean cup."

"Very clean," he said, turning to the outer door, which now rumbled open.

THIRTY-SEVEN

A MAN WITH SPIES

THE HOUSE OF Red Banners was not much more than a bed-chamber lit by a brazier lamp and warmed by an open pit irori. They sat down by the doors to take off their boots. Yamabuki's feet started to get colder, but as she walked further inside, the slightly warmer darkness invited her.

He set his long sword down on a stand. She set her sheathed medium sword down to her right, taking a seat near the fire.

He lit another small brazier. The tiny orange flame gave the illusion of heat where there was little. He threw fresh coals onto the dark-red irori embers. She fixed her gaze on the hint of flame that flicked around the lumps.

"I saved this," he said, opening a large saddle bag. He reached in and withdrew not a flask, but a small cedar *taru*. "This is from Shinano," he said. "There is none better."

"You always carry a barrel of saké with you?"

He laughed. "Not as often as I would like. I was saving it for a special occasion, and I suppose this is the special occasion I was saving it for. This saké's the *best*."

Yamabuki laughed skeptically. Everywhere she had been for

the past eleven days, everyone had claimed that their saké was *ichiban*—the best in the Empire.

Easily, he removed the keg's top and dipped two cups into the ferment. Looking expectantly, he handed the brimming cup to her. The dark orange of the braziers flickered in his dark eyes filled with boyish playfulness, and unlike the broad grin he had always displayed up until now, his smile was small, with a purity she had not seen before.

"We shall drink?" he asked, his voice low.

She sipped the saké. *Sweet. Like his smile.*

He threw back his head and quaffed his cup in but a gulp. When he belched, it amused her and she allowed herself to giggle. He wiped his sleeve across his mouth. "Ah!" he growled. "There is nothing like the saké from home."

She looked at him and he laughed at himself. She had to admit that his saké was good indeed. She wondered if it was the cold or if it was the drink, but she could not altogether feel her lips.

The irori sputtered as the coals caught fire. The light changed from the cozy orange to a brighter yellow.

He sat down. " I can't place your accent, but it is clear you have spent some time at the High Court," he said.

"Oh," she sounded amused. "A student of languages?"

"A student of people." He looked up. "I have a confession."

"Confessing already?"

"I saw your clan crest of crossed-feathers."

"Then you have me at the disadvantage. I am unfamiliar with the gentian flower the way you display it."

"I was born in Musashi Prefecture, if that's what you are asking, but I grew up in Shinano Prefecture amongst the Nakahara clan."

"Shinano, the source of the saké, of course," she said, feeling the warmth of the fire.

"I am Minamoto Yoshinaka. May I learn your name?"

"A Minamoto," she said, duly impressed as she sipped more saké. "We are already exchanging names, then, are we? I hope this does not mean that you want to duel."

"Hardly."

"I am Taka Yamabuki."

"But not an ordinary samurai."

"Why do you say that?"

"Everything about you."

"Everything?"

"Everything," he said emphatically as he quaffed down another saké. He stood up, got the taru, and set it down between them.

She gave the barrel a long look. "I don't think we can drink *that* much."

He laughed politely and continued speaking seriously, "You have been well trained. You have considerable control."

"Oh?" she said simply. "Another divination."

"Not a divination. A deduction."

She tilted her head.

"By how you handled those five back there. Someone unskilled— younger—would have drawn steel either to prove themselves or because they were scared. I've seen that kind of mistake before. The inexperienced ones always bring far too much force to a situation. They kill when a simple rap on the knuckles is sufficient to make the point."

"Yes." She smiled darkly. "And you are *so* experienced that you merely sat there and did nothing."

"Why would I get in your way? I came to the saké house to see you."

"That I do not believe. You were already there when I came in."

"Yes, I had been there for some time, waiting for you to arrive."

She gave him a crooked smile. "You just sit around saké houses, waiting for people to arrive?"

"No. Just you."

"Just me?"

"I have my spies."

"Ah, a man with spies. You must cast quite the net."

"That boy you encountered when you rode in today?"

"The half-wit in the undersized tunic?"

"He's no half-wit. Actually he is quite bright. He merely has the misfortune of having been born Unagi's son. However, right after you arrived in town, he came here and described you perfectly."

"It is good to be perfect."

"He said: a magnificent woman warrior has arrived. A tai-shōgun. But it turned out you were only Taka."

"Only Taka." She forced a deep sigh. "I am sorry to disappoint."

"When I visited Kōno's armory, from your armor I could see that you had been in a fight for your life. Never easy, despite what the simpletons say. It is always frightening, especially after it's over. It's what I saw in your eyes when I asked if you ever had to kill someone."

"And my eyes tell you this?" She smiled darkly.

"No. Your armor."

"My armor? I am not wearing armor."

"Oh, you are wearing an armor of its own sort. Behind the face you hide, a woman of breeding prowls."

"Humph."

"Ah! It was Kōno who said the rent in your armor came from such a nodachi." He leaned forward. "You stepped in, didn't you?"

She said nothing.

"Ha! I knew it! You did. We all learn *that one* in training, but few have the daring to actually do it."

"Dare or die," she said quietly.

"Most die," he responded, just as quietly. "There's what they teach, and yes, we learn that, but when there is someone else— someone who truly wishes you harm—it's another matter."

"It's easier," she said.

"How is it easier?"

Yamabuki downed a draught of saké. "In training I always had trouble imagining an opponent who was frightening . . . picturing it, I mean. In real life, though, it is easy to see what and who you are fighting and why. The moves become as drilled in—" She stopped. "I'm not sure why I am saying all this to you. I don't know you."

"Don't you?" He paused. "How old are you?"

"I am nineteen springs," she said.

"As am I," he said quickly. "I was barely fourteen springs when I had a duel in which my opponent did not survive. He was older. A man twice my years. Roku. Tada Roku. I remember him more clearly than anyone I have fought since . . . better than those five who attacked me at Waxing Moon. Those five? They announced their names and everything, and to tell you the truth, I forgot them as soon as I heard them. Nobodies who decided to kill me. But Tada Roku?" He paused with a deep sigh. "His name I shall never forget."

Yoshinaka stopped. He had spoken of something he had never

spoken about before. It was now Yamabuki's turn to likewise expose herself.

There was a long silence.

"I killed two in the battle today. The first one"—she paused, thinking on Yoshinaka's words—"I am not even sure of his true name. An assassin dressed as a monk who called himself Akibō. I got him in the shoulder. The lung. I kept fighting his fellow assassin. When that ended, I looked over. Akibō was dead." She shook her head. "Face down. All the blood was out of him. I didn't think a person had so much blood in them. Still, I don't know why I am telling you all this."

"We have something in common. It's wolves recognizing wolves."

"Nakagawa called it that," Yamabuki said.

Yoshinaka grinned. "It is something that is certainly known outside of the Taka circles. We are all wolves, even women wolves, and the life of the wolf is a lonely one. Solitary, even when we run in packs like our four-legged brethren."

"More like the tiger." Yamabuki smiled darkly, pondering his words.

"Yes. Like the tiger. The solitary hunter. And being such, it can be lonely. Sometimes when one tiger meets another, they fight, and sometimes they do not." He looked at her. "Sometimes, especially if one of the tigers is a male and the other a female, there is a bond that transcends everything."

Yamabuki gave him a hard look. "*This* female tiger, as you put it, killed male tigers today. I am not sure you want to pursue that parable."

Yoshinaka laughed. "And did I not mention that female tigers must not ever be underestimated?"

Yamabuki's eyes grew narrow. "Have you ever been betrayed?" Her voice was soft.

Yoshinaka snorted, "Of course! Before I was born."

She cocked her head. "*Before* you were born?"

He laughed. "I was in my mother's womb. My father was killed. Our lands, taken. Those loyal to me were put to the sword."

Yamabuki was dismayed at the thought. "That is a large number."

He poured her another cup of saké. "Is that so surprising? he asked.

"Are you looking to avenge your father?"

"It was my uncle who did it, but he was assassinated when I was still small."

Yamabuki shook her head. "But your own family?"

"Power is a strange thing, and for power, people will destroy their own flesh and blood, and all too often themselves in the process. I suppose you grew up amongst the Taka without ever giving your clan's continued existence another thought," he said. "After my young uncle killed my father, I was spared because I was newborn. I was sent away to be raised by another clan who took pity on my mother and me. Later my uncle decided he wanted to kill me anyway. But he died first." Yoshinaka's intensity lingered. "I foolishly thought that after that, all I had to do was retake my rightful place as daimyō, but his son, my cousin, stepped in as daimyō. Banishment has a finality." He gave her a sly look. "Unless, of course, you gather an army and take back your birthright."

"Losing a birthright is hard to imagine." She paused.

"It sets things into motion that changes your life and you spend the rest of your days struggling with the loss, whether you decide to reclaim it or not." All the glowing boyishness was now gone, replaced by a person who carried a heavy burden.

She looked at him for a long moment. In answer she said, "It does not always work that way. Being deprived is terrible, but all things have a secret side that no one but the person living through it can ever fully understand. Being chosen as the next daimyō has its own special pains. Most everyone gleefully imagines how wonderful it would be to have that kind of power, yet it is like riding the tiger's back. Once there, you dare not let go. And you must always remember to sleep with one eye open."

He poured them both another drink. "Loss lets you see how easy it is to topple something that looks so strong and mighty." His eyes shined. "Ever play jackstraws?"

She nodded. "A child's game."

"The kind of jackstraws that is played by people of our age and birth is the jackstraws of empires."

Yamabuki looked at him suspiciously.

"You? Taka. Fujiwara, yes?" he asked.

Yamabuki nodded. "Most directly through my mother—the Itō side. She reminded me of that on Dark Moon's Night, last, just before I left Ō-utsumi Prefecture."

"And *I* am Minamoto!" he said, teeth flashing. "Both of us from royal houses . . . after all, aren't all the kuge? We're all related. Any one of us could rule."

She studied him silently.

"We could topple the rulers," he said quietly, raising his saké bowl as if he and she were taking vows, but they weren't.

Yamabuki gave him a skeptical look. "The Emperor is a living God. You would be wise not to try to topple Him."

"Who said anything about the Emperor? We serve Him. He who serves the Emperor, rules, yes?"

The conversation was not to her liking. When she had entered his chamber, she felt no fear of him. He had seemed innocent. She had even fleetingly suspected their evening together would end up like the previous night, when it was Ryuma who held her in his powerful arms. But now she grew fearful—not of him physically—but of what he was saying.

What is this man capable of? His thoughts and words were dangerous.

"We have drunk a lot."

"The keg is hardly touched," he said brightly.

"I must be going." Yamabuki shifted uneasily.

"Just a moment more, and forgive me for asking. It was not idle conversation when *you* asked about betrayal." He was choosing his words carefully.

She looked at him with renewed interest. "Why do you say that?"

He held her gaze. "It sounds like you only started on your journey recently. You were it a battle just this morning against assassins. It's hard to imagine you would have generated so many enemies so quickly. Obviously someone sent them. Someone who knew you were traveling. Someone who would be better off if you were eliminated here on the Main Isle so that your disappearance might never be explained."

"Maybe," she said softly.

"Of course you don't need to answer, but I am sure others of the Taka knew when you left. Easy enough for someone to start some mischief."

She looked down glumly at the meaning behind his words. "The assassins knew some quite specific things. Things known only to a few."

"May I ask who knew?"

She paused to think. What did it matter? If this man were an assassin, he would have already struck. What he had on his mind was not a duel. "My father, my mother, my tutor, and my handmaids are the only ones who knew. No one else. Not even my bodyguards."

"Is your father in good stead with the daimyō?"

"He *is* the daimyō!"

"Ha!" Yoshinaka exclaimed. "I am not surprised. Who is next in succession? Your brother?"

"I am."

He nodded. "So we are the same in this, too. No wonder there are those who would thwart you. So it's either your tutor or the handmaids or some combination who betrayed you."

Yamabuki expelled a deep breath. She was drunk and had been careless in her words. "I must go. The night is late."

"Very well, Taka-sama." He smiled. "Maybe we will see each other before we part in our separate directions."

She picked up her sword and rose surprisingly unsteadily to her feet.

"I will stop by the armory first thing in the morning." He grinned. "Maybe just to say farewell."

She steadied herself as she got to the door. "Too bad I'll miss you. I'll be asleep."

THIRTY-EIGHT

I'll Settle Some Scores

S HE STEPPED INTO the night, where the cold mountain air revived her. It was dark. The chill cut through her. She shivered despite her resolve to hide her discomfort. Snow started to fall— tiny flakes smaller than sand, the kind that quickly piled up.

She watched her breath steam as she headed down the quiet lane toward the armory, her arms crossed over her chest and tucked into the kimono sleeves for warmth, her fingers touching the three scrolls and her dagger. She thought of Blue Rice, who that morning had carried his saké in his sleeve in much the same manner.

She asked herself, if these same events had happened the night before, would she would have reacted in the same way as she just had? Not just at the House of Red Banners, but also with the five guards. Perhaps not, but that was yesterday.

Tonight was she so full of saké that she felt it necessary to break their bones? Was it that she was tired? Or angry? Or was it that compared to the morning's killings, this was a small matter that had to be settled then and there or the louts might have come back for more?

After the duel at the Shintō shrine, she had looked at her eyes' reflection in her blade. She had convinced herself that her she had not changed, and yet Yoshinaka claimed that he could see she had killed. And if he didn't see it in her eyes, then he saw it in her actions. Was there any difference in how he knew? She was revealing it without thinking.

She looked up and down the empty streets wondering if any of the sakimori might indeed be lurking somewhere, waiting for the chance to have another go after all. Maybe they would bring lieutenant Misaki with them.

Then I'll settle some scores.

She sensed that she smiled wickedly. But if that is what she hoped, she was disappointed. Not so much as a dog nor a fox yelped.

When she arrived at the main armory building, she noticed that light leaked from the cracks in its shuttered windows and doors. Someone surely was working into the night.

She walked along, leaving tracks in the fresh snow. She continued on around and entered the guest quarters, knocking her boots to get the slush off. Thankfully a small lamp burned inside the entryway, lighting the two steps into the chamber where she was to sleep.

By the light of the brazier, she sat before the little, polished steel mirror on the low stand. She looked at her face and at her white make-up.

She considered the five sakimori. *They did not recognize me.*

A pinewood bucket with fresh water had been placed next to the stand. With a small damp towel, she removed the rice-white make-up. The singular smell of the wet rice filled the room.

She dried her face, then brushed her wet tresses. *Tangled.* Life on the road had its share of hardships, but it was not as if she hadn't been warned. Her mother had warned her about everything, even what would happen if Yamabuki found herself embroiled in combat.

Lady Taka had said, before Yamabuki set out, "Because blossoms are beautiful, there are those who will seek to tear them off their branches."

THIRTY-NINE

THE LAKE OF DREAMS

A T LAST, YAMABUKI turned down the brazier and, for the eleventh night, slept in a strange room, this night alone. She closed her eyes. Her head spun. She was falling asleep when she heard a small tapping at the door to her chamber. Would Yoshinaka be so crass as to have followed her? Warrior or not, this would not go well for him. She smoothly slid her left hand to Tiger Cub's hilt and gripped its leather and silk windings. With her thumb, she pushed, loosening the blade very slightly from its scabbard.

Next came a tiny giggle. It was that of a small girl.

"Kouma?" Yamabuki whispered.

Another giggle. Was the girl was already inside? If so, she had slipped in ever so softly.

Yamabuki said, "You're up late. Does your father know you are walking about in the night?"

"No," a voice answered tentatively.

"When I was your age if I had been caught wandering around in the Hour of the Ox, my father would have been quite cross with me."

"You are afraid," Kouma said in a small voice.

"Oh?" Yamabuki replied in a voice equally soft.

"You're afraid people will hurt you. And you have to hurt them instead."

Yamabuki wondered if that was true.

Kouma giggled and said, "Those were bad men and you scolded them good."

"At the saké house?"

The girl giggled again.

My what a small town. Word travels fast. Even children know things within an hour of them happening.

The little girl's voice came closer. "This is a good place. My father likes you. You will sleep. No bad dreams."

No bad dreams. Yamabuki laughed softly to herself.

The girl moved through the shadows. Yamabuki thought she heard the door slide aside as Kouma softly left the chamber. Yamabuki was alone and too tired to open the door to see where Kouma went. Instead, she wandered ever deeper into a dream state. She saw the fencing master, Shima, though not as she saw him in death. He wore the same indigo and orange armor, carried his nodachi, and displayed the *hanabishi* clan symbol. He seemed pleased to see her.

"*Death walks the road,*" he said in the dream. "*Saburo will be here soon.*"

"Let him come . . ." she heard herself say. She would rest for now. She was deliciously drunk. Happily she fell further into a very deep, profound, and peaceful sleep.

NOTE ON JAPANESE NAMES AND WORDS

This is a novel of English language fiction, which takes place in the twelfth century. In the wider world it is the time of the first Plantagenet kings, the era of Henry II and Becket. Gaelic Ireland is about to be invaded by the Normans. The Magna Carta is decades away. People speak *Beowulf* English. The discovery of the Americas by western Europeans remains 300 years in the future.

Just as England was not yet the England of Shakespeare, Japan was remarkably different from the Japan of the Tokugawa era. For many of us in the West, our impressions of what ancient Japan might have been like often come from motion pictures. *Ran, Seven Samurai, Yojimbo, Zatoichi, Throne of Blood, Hara-Kiri, Sword of Doom, Lone Wolf and Cub*, and even the American TV film *Shogun* come to mind. While historically faithful, most are set in the late-sixteenth century and after. We picture two-sword samurai with shaved pates, seductive geisha, kabuki theater, Nō drama, hara-kiri ritual suicides, communal baths, tea drinking and tea ceremonies, and Zen Buddhism—none of which were part of the twelfth century.

That does not mean that the era of Yamabuki was bland. To the contrary. That was when Lady Murasaki Shikibu, "Japan's Shakespeare," wrote *The Tale of Genji*. The Yamabuki stories take place in the rich Heian era, a time when arts, music, and poetry still flourished, and great armies marched in epic battles in the pursuit of mastery over the Empire. It was a time when the station of women was high, when women were not only great writers and poets, but when females dared to be warriors, and when there even was a female shogun.

In keeping with the Japanese language, Japanese words used are not stated in the conventional plural (by adding "s"). Thus, for example, "neko" in Japanese means cat, cats, a specific cat, cats in general, or some cats. The author tries to be consistent in this throughout the book.

Names are faithful to the Japanese custom of surname first, then any royal title, and finally personal name(s).

Time is expressed in the twelve zodiac hours—six hours of daylight and six hours of dark, irrespective of the season—each hour being equivalent to more or less two modern western hours. Additionally, there are five two-hour periods, "watches," during the night. The Fourth Watch, the time from 1 AM to 3 AM, is the Hour of the Ox, the witching hour.

Months and seasons are reckoned by the twelve months of the lunar calendar, with the first day of the year usually falling somewhere in late January or early February. Every few years, a thirteenth month is added to keep the lunar calendar aligned with the corrects growing seasons.

The seven-day week was not known, nor was the concept of a "dozen," per se. Neither were miles, yards, feet, inches. Nor is time broken down into minutes and seconds in the way we think of it today.

KML
Boulder Colorado
November 2015
Akahito 26

CHARACTERS, GLOSSARY, AND REFERENCE

CHARACTERS

Akibō: An assassin disguised as a monk.

Arinari: Swordsmith in Heian-kyō.

Atsumichi: Yamabuki's cousin, son of Tachibana.

Blue Rice: A traveler to Honshu; aka Aoi Ine.

Eiji: Kōno's son.

Fusa-ichi: Musician to the Taka Court.

Fuyuki: Kōno's son.

Gankyū: Nickname for Saburo; eyeball *(literal)*.

General Moroto: Lord Taka. Yamabuki's titular father.

Hachiman: The War God.

Hanaye: Yamabuki's second handmaid; excellent blessed *(literal)*.

Hiromoto: The Ōe warlord.

Iebō: An assassin disguised as a monk.

Inu: The innkeeper of Wakatake; dog *(literal)*. Member of the Yūkū family.

Jingū: Ancient Empress, mother of Hachiman.

Kiri: Saburo's housemaid.

Kōken: An empress of ancient Japan.

Kōno Taro: Armorer in Minezaki.

Lady Taka: General Moroto's wife and Yamabuki's mother.

Long Sword: An Ōuchi fencing master; aka Shima Sa-me.

Maho: A farmer selling cloth.

Mari: Kōno's daughter.

Misaki: Surname of a Nagato sakimori lieutenant; three blossoms *(literal)*.

Mochizuki: Yamabuki's horse; full moon *(literal)*.

Nakagawa: Yamabuki's tutor; middle river *(literal)*.

Obā-san: A farmer; grandma *(literal)*.

Oji-san: A farmer; uncle *(literal)*.

Rei: One of Lady Taka's handmaids.

Ryuma: A guard at Wakatake; winged horse *(literal)*.

Sa-ye: A teenage farmer girl.

Saburo: An expert assassin pursuing Yamabuki.

Shima Sa-me: Ōuchi sword master; Shark Island *(literal)*.

Tachibana: General Moroto's younger brother and Yamabuki's uncle.

Tada Roku: The first man Yoshinaka killed.

Tetsu: A kobune captain; iron *(literal)*.

Tomoko: Yamabuki's personal handmaid; wisdom *(literal)*.

Unagi: The Minezaki saké house man; eel *(literal)*.

Yamabuki: Yellow rose *(literal)*.

Yo-aki: Pseudonym of a Taka traitor; strange mystic *(literal)*.

Yo-ichi: Kōno's stable keeper; big number one *(literal)*.

Yoshinaka: A dispossessed kuge prince temporarily residing in Minezaki.

Yukiyasu: Master swordsmith to the Taka clan.

Yuma: Tachibana's first wife.

GLOSSARY

Akamagaseki: City in Nagato on Honshu, across the Barrier Strait from Kita.

Akitsushima: Ancient name of Japan; Autumn Creek Land *(literal)*.

amigasa: Braided straw hat.

awabi: Abalone.

Barrier Strait: The Kanmon Strait.

benibana: Ruby-red dye used to color cheeks and lips.

buké: Warrior; equivalent to bushi.

Bungo Strait: The Hinde-Exit Strait.

buri: Yellowtail, or amberjack.

bushi: Warrior; equivalent to buké.

Chikuzen Province: Northwestern-most district of the Isle of Unknown Fire, bordered on north by the Kanmon Strait.

chō: Thick eyebrows drawn high on the forehead, above the natural browline; butterflies *(literal)*.

daimyō: Ruler of hereditary landholdings; often translated as Lord.

Denka: Your Majesty.

dō: Armor breastplate.

dojo: Martial arts training studio.

engawa: An outer walkway of a building.

fugu: Puffer fish.

gagaku: Chinese music preferred by Japanese royalty.

Genpei War: Japanese Civil War of 1180–1185; also spelled Gempei.

genpuku: Coming-of-age ceremony for twelve-year-old boys. At this age, a boy was considered an adult.

gimi: Honorific suffix meaning "princess."

Great Bay province: Mythical province near present-day Miyazaki and Kagoshima. Home of the Taka clan.

haguro: Teeth blackening, a tradition practiced by married women, and some men.

hai: Yes.

hakama: Split trouser-skirt worn over the kimono, commonly worn by the upper classes in this era.

hanabishi: Fire flower; the Ōuchi mon.

Hayakawa: A clan of Sagani Prefecture.

Heian-kyō: The capital of Akitsushima; site of present-day Kyoto.

ichiban: Best.

ine: Rice plant.

irrashai: Welcome *(informal)*.

irrashimase: Welcome *(formal)*.

irori: Fire pit within a house.

Isle of Two Kingdoms: Ancient name of Shikoku.

Isle of Unknown Fire: Ancient name of Kyushu.

jūnihitoe: Elegant, highly complex kimono worn only by court ladies.

kabuto: Warrior helmet.

kago: Palanquin.

kaiki shoho: Gold coins.

kami: Spirits worshipped in Shintō.

kami-dana: Household shrine.

kani: Crabs.

kanji: Chinese pictogram calligraphy.

Kanmon Strait: Strait between Honshu and Kyushu.

kanzashi: Hair-band crown.

karaginumo: T'ang-style sheath and skirt composed of multiple kimono layers.

Katchū-shi: Armor maker.

kibi: Millet.

kichō: Drapes.

Kita: City at the Barrier Strait, in Chikuzen.

kobune: Water craft, used to ferry passengers and property.

kōjin-biwa: A stringed instrument.

kozane: Scales.

kuge: Aristocracy.

kugutsu: Puppet.

kuma: Bear.

kushi: Drink made from fermented barley; mysterious thing *(literal)*.

kuso: Shit *(colloquial)*.

kyōfū: Gale; strong wind *(literal)*.

Leeward Sea: Body of water known today as the Sea of Japan.

Main Isle: Honshu.

mempo: Facial armor worn by samurai in battle.

mifune: Boat.

misu: Screens.

miyage: Souvenir.

mizu: Water.

Mizuka: Significant trading city on the Isle of Unknown Fire, on the road to the Barrier Strait.

mochi gome: Sticky rice.

moe kusa: Burning herb to treat infection.

mogi: Coming-of-age ceremony for girls; adult clothes *(literal)*.

mon: Crest or symbol representing a clan.

Musashi Prefecture: Ancient Japanese prefecture.

mushi: Bedbugs.

Nagato: Province on the Main Isle, located on the Barrier Strait, across from Kita. Part of modern-day Yamaguchi Prefecture.

naginata: Polearm with a sword blade attached.

Nakahara: Clan that raised Yoshinaka from infancy.

New Life Month: A spring month also known as *U no hara*.

ninja: Hired agent, often an assassin.

nodachi: Field sword; a very long, heavy battle sword.

noshi: Small origami worn at ceremonies.

nurude: Paste made of rust, stale saké vinegar, and ground nuts used for haguro, the blackening of teeth.

nyōbō: Handmaid(s).

Ō-Utsumi Prefecture: Great Bay province, Yamabuki's home.

Ōe: Clan in Nagato.

ōgane: Largest and deepest temple bell.

Oji or **Ojisan**: Term of affection toward an elder man; uncle *(literal)*.

Omiki: Saké that's offered to the Gods.

origami: The Japanese art of folding paper into intricate designs.

oshiroi: White rice-powder make-up.

Ōuchi: Clan on the Isle of Unknown Fire.

pillow book: A diary.

pole arm: Weapon on a pole.

Qin: Ancient name of China.

Raijin: The Storm God.

reiu: Cold rain.

ryō: Gold coin currency unit.

Sagami Prefecture: Home of the Hayakawa clan.

sakimori: Historical name for border guards.

sama: Honorific when addressing a superior.

samisen: A Japanese guitar with three strings.

san: Polite salutation, equal to Mister or Miss.

senchou: Boat chief.

Shinano Prefecture: A 12th-century province.

Shinmoe-dake: Volcanic mountain on the Isle of Unknown Fire.

shinobi: Ninja.

shitagi: Under-sheath, underwear.

shitagasane: Kimono train.

shōben: To piss, urinate.

Sòng Dynasty: Ancient Chinese dynasty.

sumi: Ink stick.

tachi: Long sword commonly worn by samurai.

tai-shōgun: Big military commander.

Taka: Yamabuki's clan; hawk *(literal)*.

tantō: Dagger.

taru: Barrel.

Tendai sect: A Buddhist sect.

Tennō: Majesty *(honorific)*.

tessen: War fan made out of metal.

Tiger Claw: Name of Yamabuki's tachi.

Tiger Cub: Name of Yamabuki's medium-length personal sword.

toi: Foreign; Korean.

tomoe: A circular pin-wheel symbol.

tōsō: The pox.

tsurigane: A medium-sized hanging bell.

Tsukushi: Another ancient name for Kyushu, Yamabuki's home isle.

tsuchi: Soil.

Wakatake: An inn in Kita; young bamboo *(literal)*.

Wéi-Qí: [Chinese] The game of Go.

Windward Sea: Pacific Ocean.

yahochi: Prostitute.

yoroi: Full armor.

JAPANESE YEARS, SEASONS, AND TIME

SOLAR STEMS

	Romanji	*Kanji*	*Start Date*	*Name*
1	**Risshun**	立春	February 4	Beginning of spring
2	**Usui**	雨水	February 18	Rain water
3	**Keichitsu**	啓蟄	March 5	Awakening of Insects
4	**Shunbun**	春分	March 20	Vernal equinox
5	**Seimei**	清明	April 4	Clear and bright
6	**Kokuu**	穀雨	April 20	Grain rain
7	**Rikka**	立夏	May 5	Beginning of summer
8	**Shōman**	小満	May 21	Grain Fills
9	**Bōshu**	芒種	June 5	Grain in Ear
10	**Geshi**	夏至	June 21	Summer Solstice
11	**Shōsho**	小暑	July 7	Little Heat
12	**Taisho**	大暑	July 23	Great Heat
13	**Risshū**	立秋	August 7	Beginning of Autumn
14	**Shosho**	処暑	August 23	End of Heat
15	**Hakuro**	白露	September 7	Descent of White Dew
16	**Shūbun**	秋分	September 23	Autumnal Equinox
17	**Kanro**	寒露	October 8	Cold Dew
18	**Sōkō**	霜降	October 23	Descent of Frost
19	**Rittō**	立冬	November 7	Beginning of winter
20	**Shōsetsu**	小雪	November 22	Little Snow
21	**Taisetsu**	大雪	December 7	Great Snow
22	**Tōji**	冬至	December 22	Winter Solstice
23	**Shōkan**	小寒	January 5	Little Cold
24	**Daikan**	大寒	January 20	Great Cold

JAPANESE YEARS

Kiūan 1–6   Jan 25, 1145 to Jan 19, 1151
Kiūan 5 has a 13th month observed starting July 18, 1148

Nimbiō 1–3   Jan 20, 1151 to Feb 13, 1154
Nimbiō 1 has a 13th month observed starting May 18, 1151
Nimbiō 3 has a 13th month observed starting Jan 16, 1154

Kiūju 1–2   Feb 14, 1154 to Jan 20, 1156

Hōgen 1–3   Jan 21, 1156 to Jan 20, 1159
Hōgen 1 has a 13th month observed starting Oct 16, 1156

Heiji 1   Jan 21, 1159 to Feb 8, 1160
Heiji 1 has a 13th month observed starting June 18, 1159

Eiriaku 1   Feb 9, 1160 to Jan 27, 1161

Ōhō 1–2   Jan 28, 1161 to Feb 4, 1163
Ōhō 2 has a 13th month observed starting April 17, 1162

Chōkwan 1–2   Feb 5, 1163 to Feb 12, 1165
Chōkwan 2 has a 13th month observed starting Dec 16, 1164

Eiman 1   Feb 13, 1165 – Feb 2, 1166

Nin-an 1–3   Feb 3, 1166 to Jan 29, 1169
Nin-an 2 has a 13th month observed starting August 17, 1167

Kaō 1–2   Jan 30, 1169 to Feb 6, 1171

Shōan 1–4   Feb 7, 1171 to Jan 23, 1175
Shōan 2 has a 13th month observed starting January 16, 1173

Angen 1–2   Jan 24, 1175 to Jan 31, 1177
Angen 1 has a 13th month observed starting October 17, 1175

JAPANESE HOURS

Hour	Bell Strikes	Solar time
Rabbit	6	5 – 7 AM
Dragon	5	7 – 9 AM
Snake	4	9 – 11 AM
Horse	9	11 AM – 1 PM *(Noon)*
Sheep	8	1 – 3 PM
Monkey	7	3 – 5 PM
Bird	6	5 – 7 PM
Dog – *Shokō, First Watch*	5	7 – 9 PM
Pig – *Nikō, Second Watch*	4	9 – 11 PM
Mouse – *Saukō, Third Watch*	9	11 PM – 1 AM *(Midnight)*
Ox – *Shikō, Fourth Watch*	8	1 – 3 AM *("witching hour")*
Tiger – *Gokō, Fifth Watch*	7	3 – 5 AM

NOTE: The hours of the day are defined as divisions of time between sunrise and sunset, and back to sunrise again. There are six Japanese hours in each day and six each night. The sun always rises in the Hour of the Rabbit, and sets in the Hour of the Bird. Naturally, as the seasons change, nighttime and daytime hours will vary in actual duration, daytime hours longer during the summer, nighttime hours longer during the winter. Averaged out over the year, each "hour" works out to be approximately two of our modern hours.

If you enjoyed Cold Rain . . .

. . . please consider posting a brief review online
to help others discover the book. Thank you!

EXTRAS

Excerpt from Cold Heart: Yamabuki vs. the Ninja
(Sword of the Taka Samurai, Book Three)

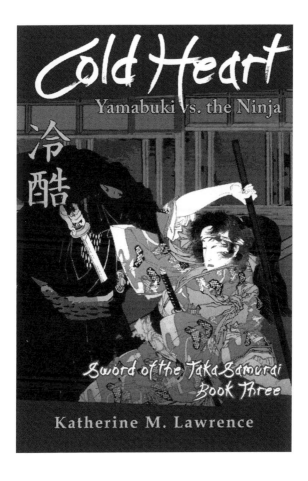

THE UNMET FRIEND

A DAMP CHILL FILLED the mountains during the nineteenth solar stem, Ritto: that season when dead trees cannot be distinguished from the living; when pungent, hot hearth smoke mixes with cool mists that wander through forests; when darkness intrudes early and dawn breaks late.

Saburo gazed from the monastery's main entry-gate window, contemplating the waning half-moon as it began to slowly set in the tranquility of the late afternoon. Most of the familiar birds had flown away to who knew where. Now and then, only the squawking geese, flying in large formations, broke the stillness. Other than that, the calm was disturbed only by the wind which set the leafless trees to creak and the evergreens to whisper. If the sun shone at all during the austere days of impending winter, the sky glowed with a trace of fading embers.

Few travelers took the route over the Dragon's Back this late in the year. Only the most dedicated would brave the pass when there was a chance of snow, and thus the roads grew quiet, and only the fool-hardy, or those running away from something or someone, would trek on down the highway from the mountain pass in waning light.

The last shadows thrown by the still-setting sun were long. It was out of one day's dying fire that a lone samurai approached the monastery on foot. Saburo watched the stranger. He knew that with the fast-falling darkness, the samurai would in all likelihood stop at the gate, for it was the custom—nay the duty—of temples to welcome travelers for the night. Likewise, travelers understood that a small donation of money, or something of value paid in-kind would help ensure a warm place to sleep and a share of the meal.

A tall and imposing man, the lone warrior drew near. He hefted a naginata over his shoulder and carried a tachi-style long sword as he walked under the weight of full yoroi battle armor. Not some lowly spearman, this. The samurai did not wear a kabuto and so Saburo could see the man's wild black mane of hair, which fell to his shoulders, framing a noble face that was bearded, rugged, and handsome in the way of men, with pronounced, yet well-proportioned, masculine features.

As custom dictated, the samurai paused before the entry gate to rinse out his mouth, then clapped his hands to alert the Gods, as well as everyone else, that he had arrived and intended to enter.

Saburo decided he could no longer lurk in the shadows, so he stepped forward and opened the entry.

The samurai's dark eyes, like a tiger's, scanned Saburo, but not with hostility, nor malevolence. More, they were curious, looking perhaps for something. The samurai might well have been wondering what sort of order he had encountered, what kind of monks lived here, and what customs would be observed. He was perhaps ten years older and at least a head taller and certainly wider than Saburo.

"How did you get this duty, squinting into the setting sun?" asked the warrior, his voice deep and sonorous.

Saburo frowned, not sure what the man was asking.

"I saw you lurking behind the gate," the man said at last. "The sun lit you up. It was in your eyes, but it was at my back. My advantage." He sniffed as he set his naginata down, then sat down at the threshold to remove his traveling shoes—bearskin boots, at that. The man smiled. Had the warrior noticed Saburo's awe at something so simple as footwear?

Saburo felt himself flush. A first-level priest was not supposed to feel this sort of admiration. Priests were men of peace while samurai were men of combat.

The man removed his haori, a kind of field coat, revealing battle-worn red armor that had been patched and repaired. Saburo tried not to gape, but clearly the mending meant that the stranger had seen the thick of the fighting and had survived; but most impressive of all was his insignia: Imperial. No question. The samurai had fought on behalf of the Emperor, the Son of Heaven himself.

The man finally broke the silence. "You have a name?"

"I'm Dankotaru," Saburo said, giving his formal, priestly name—one he rarely used.

"Are you?"

"Am I what?"

"'Resolute.' Like your name says."

Saburo still felt awkward and wasn't sure what to say. There was something about this winning man that drew Saburo to him. He was powerful, yet calm. Likely he could be fierce if needed, but yet he spoke with an unruffled coolness.

"I'm called Shima Sa-me," the samurai offered. This was

uncharacteristic, for samurai did not offer their names to those who were not at least of the buké class. Perhaps he respected Saburo's status as a priest. "You always called Dankotaru?"

Saburo shook his head.

"I didn't think so. Long name. What did they call you before you came to the temple?" Shima asked.

"Gankyū."

"Eyeball?"

"Hai." Saburo nodded.

Shima said, standing up, "My name means 'Island Shark.' Where can I find something to eat? You have meat?"

Saburo shook his head. "We have taken vows not to kill, so we eat only grains and vegetables. Sometimes fruit. Most of what we have now's been dried."

"Hmm." Shima sighed. "Religion means you have to give up a lot."

"Actually, even if it were allowed, we're too poor to afford it, so if we make it a religious rule, like the Buddhists do, it comes out righteous."

Shima laughed—a bellow that resonated from deep inside. "I like you, Gun-kun."

Saburo pondered the name Shima had just given him, a mispronunciation of the hateful name "Gankyū." Shima had turned "Gan" into "Gun," which on its own meant "soldier," and "kyū" into "kun," a form of respect used among young men—one which was usually shared among comrades. Saburo felt flattered.

"Gun-kun? Any saké?" Shima asked slyly.

Saburo considered the risk of taking saké from the storehouse—saké used for sacred rites. Yet he wanted to please this warrior who was being so friendly. He whispered, "I think I know where I can find some."

"Where are the other priests?"

"At prayers. It's the observance of the first night of winter. I think I can find some roots to eat."

"Roots!" Shima almost spat the word. "Roots and saké?" Shima shuddered. "How about fresh rabbit?"

"Rabbit?"

"You think these are only for war?" Shima pointed at his arrows. "Is there a place we can set up a cook fire, away from all the prayers? We'll eat rabbit and drink saké. And I'll talk . . . I can see you want to hear about the Ran." said Shima.

"You fought in the Hōgen Ran?" Saburo bit his lip, trying to quiet the excitement he felt.

"You were looking at all the scuffs on my armor. Let's find that quiet place, and if eating rabbit offends your religion, you can just drink the saké. I'll tell you about the battles last summer."

The two went to a place up the hill behind the temple, where the smoke and smell of the fire and cooking rabbit would not drift down to the priests' noses.

And the saké worked well in surfacing Shima's recollections. As his saké cup overflowed, so too did he overflow with stories, all of which the young priest believed as much as any holy writ he had ever embraced at Rock River Temple. The stories were all about sword fighting and enemies falling, heroes, triumph, and how the forces of the rightful Emperor crushed those who followed a treasonous path.

Shima offered, "Young men no older than yourself distinguished themselves in single combat."

Saburo hung on every word.

Shima continued, "Combat does not know rank. Someone lower in the social order, if he's trained or just plain lucky, can defeat someone of a higher station. It's said, 'A man can come to battle as a farmer and leave as a general.'"

Shima quaffed more saké with each recollection.

"A thousand fell. And by the end of the fighting, the heads of at least fifty enemy captains found their way to the points of pikes and were put on display, six of whom I personally defeated."

Saburo, in a tactful way, asked why if Shima was so illustrious did he not stay in Heian-kyō. He feared his question might insult the mighty Shima, but instead Shima's voice grew soft. "The trouble with winning is that there is never enough reward to go around for the victors, and everyone is a hero. Heroes who fight for no pay, but just the glory, end up with nothing. And no money. And as for the glory, no one remembers it except you yourself." Shima grinned. "The wise ones"—meaning himself—"take their skills to places where their abilities are rare and will be appreciated. Remember the old saying, 'A hero goes unsung in his own house'?" Shima laughed. "But I plan to take what I know and go to the Isle of Unknown Fires. The Ōuchi are looking for sword masters to teach their warriors. I'll be leaving in the morning. But first I need to 'go and lean'"—meaning Shima, now filled with more than his share of saké, had to relieve himself.

"Gun-kun. Want to help me with my armor?"

ABOUT TOOT SWEET INK

Toot Sweet Ink is an imprint of Toot Sweet Inc., an independent publisher based in Boulder, Colorado.

Watch for our upcoming releases in science fiction, non-fiction, women's contemporary fiction, humor, and historical fiction, including more Yamabuki stories by Katherine M. Lawrence.

Follow us on Twitter: @TootSweetInk

http://facebook.com/tootsweetink

http://TootSweet.ink

Sign up for our Inkvine newsletter to get updates and learn about new releases and discount opportunities on our upcoming titles, at eepurl.com/K8XVn

ABOUT THE AUTHOR

For several years, Katherine M. Lawrence has been researching and writing the adventures of Yamabuki, an actual historic female samurai who lived in the Heian Era of Japan. Inspired by several decades in the martial arts halls led by women—Ja Shin Do, the San Jose State University Kendo Club, and Pai Lum White Lotus Fist: Crane style—Katherine set out to write about the experiences of women who train in warriors' skills . . . and Yamabuki in particular. The first books to be published from that effort are *Cold Saké*, *Cold Blood*, and this book, *Cold Rain*.

Katherine graduated from the University of Washington with an undergraduate degree in both History and Chemistry, and continued with work on a Masters in History at the Far Eastern and Slavic Institute. She also received an MBA from Harvard University.

She is currently developing further books about the adventures of Yamabuki. She lives in Boulder, Colorado.

Kate blogs at http://KateLore.com

Follow her on Twitter: @pingkate

To get advance notifications on Kate's upcoming releases, sign up for her newsletter at http://eepurl.com/K8IIf

Printed in Great Britain
by Amazon